A man was staring at her.

Not just any man, either. He was tall, perhaps six foot one or two, with short dark hair and blue eyes, powerful muscles and a square, determined sort of jaw. He was just the sort of man who made her most nervous, the kind who didn't look as if they could be swayed by a flirty smile and a sidelong look.

He was staring at her as if she had just sprouted horns out the top of her head. She frowned, uncomfortable with his scrutiny, though she couldn't have said exactly why.

She had no clear memory of arriving here, only a vague sense that something was very wrong, that someone was supposed to help her sort everything out.

She looked at the man again, registering that he was extraordinarily handsome in a clean-cut sort of way.

Had she been looking for him? She blinked, trying to sort through the jumble of her thoughts.

Then suddenly she remembered.

Baby. The baby. Her baby.

Dear Reader,

From the very first moment I came up with the idea for my latest COWBOYS OF COLD CREEK trilogy, I fell in love with Brant Western and couldn't wait to write about him. He's deeply honorable but conflicted, grieving the loss of several people close to him and in dire need of a little peace between deployments. Part of me would have loved to give him that…but what kind of boring story would that have been? Instead, I decided to shake up his world by sending him the most unlikely of heroines, Mimi Van Hoyt—heiress, celebrity, tabloid princess du jour. Mimi is a complicated woman. Like all of us, she's made mistakes, but she's finally at a place in her life where she's ready to learn from them. From the beginning I knew she would be the perfect woman for Brant, that she would teach him to laugh again, to not take himself so seriously, to squeeze every drop of joy he could from life. I loved writing their story and helping these two people find each other!

All my best,

RaeAnne

A COLD CREEK SECRET

RAEANNE THAYNE

SPECIAL EDITION®

Published by Silhouette Books

America's Publisher of Contemporary Romance

SILHOUETTE BOOKS

ISBN-13: 978-0-373-65507-6

Recycling programs
for this product may
not exist in your area.

A COLD CREEK SECRET

Copyright © 2010 by RaeAnne Thayne

Visit Silhouette Books at www.eHarlequin.com

Printed in U.S.A.

Books by RaeAnne Thayne

RAEANNE THAYNE

finds inspiration in the beautiful northern Utah mountains, where she lives with her husband and three children. Her books have won numerous honors, including three RITA® Award nominations from Romance Writers of America and a Career Achievement Award from *RT Book Reviews* magazine. RaeAnne loves to hear from readers and can be reached through her Web site at www.raeannethayne.com.

To the wonderful writers of Utah RWA
for your support, encouragement and friendship.

Chapter One

No matter what exotic parts of the world he visited, Brant Western hadn't forgotten how the cold of a February evening in Idaho could clutch at his lungs with icy claws that refused to let go.

In the past hour, the light snow flurries of the afternoon had turned vicious, intense. The active storm front forecasters had been warning about since he arrived for his mid-tour leave two days earlier had finally started its relentless march across this tiny corner of eastern Idaho toward Wyoming.

Icy flakes spit against his unprotected face with all the force of an Al Asad sandstorm. Somehow they found their way to every exposed surface, even sliding beneath the collar of his heavy shearling-lined ranch coat.

This was the sort of Idaho night made for hunkering down by the fire with a good book and a cup of hot cocoa.

The picture had undeniable appeal, one of the many images of home that had sustained him through fierce firefights and long campaigns and endless nights under Afghan and Iraqi stars.

After, he reminded himself. When the few cattle at the Western Sky had been fed and all the horses were safe and snug in the barn, then he could settle in front of the fire with the thriller he'd picked up in the airport.

"Come on, Tag. We're almost done, then we can go home."

His horse, a sturdy buckskin gelding, whinnied as if he completely understood every word and continued plodding along the faint outline of a road still visible under the quickly falling snow.

Brant supposed this was a crazy journey. The hundred head of cows and their calves weren't even his cattle but belonged to a neighbor of the Western Sky who leased the land while Brant was deployed.

Carson McRaven took good care of his stock. Brant wouldn't have agreed to the lease if he didn't. But since the cattle were currently residing on his property, he felt responsibility toward them.

Sometimes that sense of obligation could be a genuine pain in the butt, he acknowledged as he and Tag finished making sure the warmers in the water troughs were functioning and turned back toward the house.

They hadn't gone more than a dozen yards when he saw headlights slicing weakly through the fusillade of snow, heading toward the ranch far too quickly for these wintry conditions.

He squinted in the murky twilight. Who did he know who would be stupid or crazy enough to venture out in this kind of weather?

Easton was the logical choice but he had just talked to her on the phone a half hour earlier, before he had set out on this fool's errand to check the ranch, and she had assured him that after the wedding they had both attended the night before, she was going to bed early with a lingering headache.

He worried about her. He couldn't deny that. Easton hadn't been the same since her aunt, his foster mother, had died of cancer several months earlier. Even longer, really. She hadn't been the sweet, funny girl he'd known and loved most of his life maybe since around the time Guff Winder had died.

Maybe Easton wasn't acting like herself, but he was pretty sure she had the good sense to hunker down at Winder Ranch during a storm like this. If she did venture out, he was pretty sure she was smart enough to slow down when conditions demanded it, especially since he and his foster brothers had drilled that into her head when they taught her to drive.

So if that driver wasn't Easton, who was barreling toward his ranch on the cusp of a ferocious winter storm?

Somebody lost, no doubt. Sometimes these remote canyon roads were difficult to negotiate and the snow could obscure landmarks and address markings. With a sigh, he spurred Tag toward the road to point the wayward traveler in the right direction.

He was just wishing for a decent pair of optics so he could get a better look at who it might be, when the vehicle suddenly went into a slide. He saw it coming as the driver took a curve too fast and he pushed Tag faster, praying he was wrong. But an instant later the driver overcorrected and as Brant held his breath, the vehicle spun out on the icy road.

It was almost like some grisly slow-motion movie, watching it careen over the edge of the road, heading straight for Cold Creek, at the bottom of a maybe five-foot drop.

The vehicle disappeared from view and Brant smacked the reins and dug his heels into the horse's sides, racing as fast as he dared toward the slide-out.

When he reached the creek's edge, he could barely make out in the gathering darkness that the vehicle wasn't quite submerged in the creek but it was a close thing. The SUV had landed on a large granite boulder in the middle of the creek bed, the front end crumpled and the rear wheels still on the bank.

Though he tried not to swear as a habit, he couldn't help hissing out a fierce epithet as he scrambled down from the horse. In February, the creek was only a couple feet deep at most and the current wasn't strong enough to carry off an SUV, but Brant would still have to get wet to get to the vehicle. There was no other way around it.

He heard a faint moan from inside and what sounded, oddly, like a tiny lamb bleating.

"Hang on," he called. "I'll get you out of there in a minute."

Just in the minute or two he had stood surveying the scene and figuring out how to attack the problem, darkness had completely descended and the snow stung at him from every direction. The wind surged around him, taunting and cruel. Even as cold as he was from the storm, he wasn't prepared for the frigid shock of the water through his boots and his lined Wranglers as he waded up to his knees.

He heard that moan again and this time he isolated

the sound he had mistaken for a bleating lamb. It was a dog, a tiny one by the sound of it, yipping like crazy.

"Hang on," he called. "Won't take me but a minute and I'll have you out of there, then we can call for help."

When he slogged through the water and finally reached the vehicle, he yanked open the door. The driver was female, in her mid-twenties, maybe. He had a quick impression of wisps of dark curls that looked stark in contrast with her pale, delicate features.

With every passing second, her core temperature would be dropping and he knew he needed to extract her from the SUV and out of the water and the elements before he could completely assess her condition, though it went against every basic tenet of medical training each Army Ranger received, about not moving an injury victim until you knew the extent of injuries.

"Cold," she murmured.

"I know. I'm sorry about that."

He took it as a good sign that she didn't moan or cry out when he scooped her out of the vehicle. If she had broken bones, she wouldn't have been able to hide her discomfort. She didn't say anything at all, just gripped his jacket tightly, her slight body trembling from both the shock and the cold, he guessed.

She wasn't heavy, maybe a hundred and ten pounds, he judged, but carrying her through the ice-crusted water still took every bit of his energy. By the time he reached the bank and headed up the slight slope with her in his arms, he was breathing hard and was pretty sure he couldn't feel his feet anymore.

He'd learned in the early days dealing with combat injuries that the trick to keeping injured men calm was to give as much information as he could about what was going on so they didn't feel completely out of control about what was happening to them. He figured the same technique would work just as well in accident situations. "I'm going to take you back to my place on the horse, okay?"

She nodded and didn't protest when he lifted her onto Tag's back, where she clung tightly to the pommel.

"Hang on now," he said when he was sure she was secure. "I'm going to climb on behind you and then we can get you warm and dry."

When he tried to lift his icy, wet boot into the stirrup, it seemed to weigh as much as the woman had. He had to use all his strength just to raise it that two feet. Just as he shoved it in and prepared to swing the other leg onto the horse, she gasped.

"Simone. My Simone. Please, can you get her?"

He closed his eyes. Simone must be the dog. With the wind howling around them, he couldn't hear the yips anymore and he'd been so focused on the woman that he'd completely forgotten about her dog.

"Are you okay up there for a minute?" he asked, dreading the idea of wading back through that frigid water.

"Yes. Oh, please."

He had survived worse than a little cold water, he reminded himself. Much, much worse.

Returning to the vehicle took him only a moment. In the backseat, he found at least a half-dozen pieces of luggage and a tiny pink dog carrier. The occupant yipped and growled a big show at him.

"You want to stay here?" Brant growled right back. "Because I'd be just great with that."

The dog immediately subsided and under other circumstances he might have smiled at the instant submission, if he wasn't so concerned about getting them all back to the house in one piece. "Yeah, I didn't think so. Come on, let's get you out of here."

As he considered the logistics of things, he realized there was no way he could carry the bulky dog carrier and keep hold of the woman on horseback at the same time, so he unlatched the door of the carrier. A tiny white mound of fur hurtled into his arms.

Not knowing what else to do, he unzipped his coat halfway and shoved the puffball inside then zipped his coat up again, feeling ridiculously grateful none of the men in his company could see him risking hypothermia for six pounds of fuzzy canine.

The woman was still on Tag's back, he was relieved to see when he made his torturous way back through the water, though she seemed to be slumping a little more.

She was dressed in a woefully inadequate pink parka with a fur-lined hood that looked more suited to some fancy après-ski party in Jackson Hole than braving the bitterness of an Idaho blizzard and Brant knew he needed to get them all back to the ranch house ASAP.

"Is she all right?" the woman asked.

What about him? Brant wondered grumpily. He was the one with frostbitten toes. But in answer, he unzipped his coat, where the furry white head popped out. The woman sighed in relief, her delicate features relaxing slightly, and Brant handed the dog up to her.

He caught a glimpse of the little pooch licking her face that looked oddly familiar as he climbed up behind her, but he didn't take time to analyze it as he dug his heels into the horse's side, grateful Tag was one of the strongest, steadiest horses in the small Western Sky stable.

"We'll get you warmed up. I've got a fire in the woodstove at home. Just hang on a few minutes, okay?"

She nodded, slumping back against him, and he curved his arms around her, worried she would slide off.

"Thank you," she murmured, so low he could hardly hear above the moaning of that bitter wind.

He pulled her as close as he could to block the storm as Tag trudged toward home at a hard walk, as fast as Brant dared push him.

"I'm Brant," he said after a few moments. "What's your name?"

She turned her head slightly and he saw dazed confusion in her eyes. "Where are we?" she asked instead of answering him.

He decided not to push her right now. No doubt she was still bemused from the shock of driving her SUV into a creek. "My ranch in eastern Idaho, the Western Sky. The house is just over that hill there."

She nodded slightly and then he felt her slump bonelessly against him.

"Are you still with me?" he asked with concern. When she didn't answer, his arms tightened around her. Out of pure instinct, he grabbed for the dog seconds before she would have dropped it as she slipped into unconsciousness—surely a fatal fall for the little animal from this height. He managed to snag the dog and shove it back into his coat and his arms tightened around the woman as he nudged Tag even faster.

It was a surreal journey, cold and tense and nerve-racking. He didn't see the lights of the ranch house until they had nearly reached it. When he could finally make out the solid shape of the place, Brant was quite certain it was just about the most welcome sight he had ever beheld.

He led the horse to the bottom of the porch steps and dismounted carefully, keeping a hand on the woman so she didn't teeter to the ground.

"Sorry about this, Tag," he murmured to the horse as he lifted the woman's limp form into his arms. "You've been great but I need you to hang on a few more minutes out here in the cold while I take care of our guest and then I can get you into the warm barn. You deserve some extra oats after tonight."

The horse whinnied in response as Brant rushed up the porch steps and into the house. He quickly carried her inside to the family room where, just as he'd promised, the fire he'd built up in the woodstove before he left still sent out plenty of blissful warmth.

She didn't stir when he laid her on the sofa. As he was bent over to unzip her parka so he could check her injuries, the dog wriggled free of the opening of Brant's own coat and landed on her motionless mistress and began licking her face again, where a thin line of blood trickled from a cut just above her eye.

A raspy dog's tongue was apparently enough to jolt her back to at least semiconsciousness. "Simone?" she murmured and her arms slid around the dog, who settled in the crook of her arms happily.

She was soaked through from the snow's onslaught and Brant knew she wouldn't truly warm up until he could get her out of her wet clothing. Beyond that, he had to examine her more closely for broken bones.

"I'm going to get you some dry clothes, okay? I'll be right back."

She opened her eyes again and nodded and he had the oddest sense again that he knew her. She couldn't be from around here. He was almost positive of that, but then he hadn't spent more than a few weeks at a time in Pine Gulch for fifteen years.

The bedroom he stayed in when he was here was one of the two on the main floor and from his duffel he quickly grabbed a sweatshirt and a pair of cutoff sweats that would likely probably drown her, then he returned to the family room.

"I'm going to take off your parka so I can get a better look and make sure you don't have any broken bones, okay?"

She didn't answer and he wondered if she was asleep or had slipped away again. He debated calling the Pine Gulch paramedics, but he hated to do that on a vicious night like tonight unless it was absolutely necessary. He had some medic training and could deal with most basic first aid needs. If she required more than that, he would drive her into town himself.

But he needed to assess her injuries first.

He would rather disarm a suicide bomber with his teeth than undress a semiconscious woman, but he didn't have much choice. He was only doing what had to be done, he reminded himself. Feeling huge and awkward, he pulled off what seemed pretty useless pink fur boots first, then moved the tiny dog from the woman's side to the floor. The dog easily relinquished her guard dog duties and started sniffing around the room to investigate a whole new world full of smells.

Brant unzipped the woman's parka, doing his best to ignore the soft swell of curves as he pulled the sleeves free, not an easy task since he hadn't been with a woman since before his last deployment. He was only a rescue worker here, he reminded himself. Detached and impersonal.

Her shirt had remained mostly dry under her parka,

he was relieved to discover, but her jeans were soaked through and would have to come off.

"Ma'am, you're going to have to get out of your jeans. Do you need my help or can you manage by yourself?"

"Help," she mumbled.

Naturally. He sighed and reached to unfasten the snap and zipper of her jeans. His hands brushed her waist under her soft, blue silk turtleneck. Whether his fingers were cold or whether she was reacting just to the shock of human contact, he didn't know, but she blinked a few times and scrambled away with a little cry.

The tiny dog yipped and abandoned her investigations of the room to trot over and stand protectively over her mistress, teeth bared at him as if a few pounds of fluff would do the trick to deter him.

"You need to get into dry clothes, that's all," he said, using the same calm tone he did with injured soldiers in the field. "I'm not going to hurt you, I swear. You're completely safe here."

She nodded, eyes still not fully open. As he looked at her in the full light, a memory flashed across his brain of her in some barely-there slinky red dress, tossing her dark curls and giving a sultry bedroom look out of half-closed eyes.

Crazy. He had never met the woman before in his life, he could swear to it.

He pulled her jeans off, despising himself for the little stir of interest when he found her wearing pink lacy high-cut panties.

He swallowed hard. "I'm, uh, going to check for broken bones and then I've got some sweats here we can put on you, okay?"

She nodded and watched him warily from those half-closed eyes as he ran his hands over her legs, trying to pretend she was just another of his teammates. Trouble was, Rangers didn't tend to have silky white skin and luscious curves. Or wear high-cut pink panties.

"Nothing broken that I can tell," he finally said and was relieved when he could pull the faded, voluminous sweats over her legs and hide all that delectable skin.

"Are you a doctor?" she murmured.

"Not even close. I'm in the military, ma'am. Major Brant Western, Company A, 1st Battallion, 75th Ranger Regiment."

She seemed to barely hear him but she still nodded and closed her eyes again when he tucked a blanket from the edge of the sofa around her.

Without his field experience, he might have been alarmed about her state of semiconsciousness, but he'd seen enough soldiers react just this way to a sudden shock—sort of take a little mental vacation—that he wasn't overly concerned. If she was still spacey and out of it when he came back from taking care of Tag, he would get on the horn to Jake Dalton, the only physician in Pine Gulch, and see what he recommended.

He threw a blanket over her. "Ma'am." He spoke loudly and evenly and was rewarded with those eyes opening a little more at him. He was really curious what color they were.

"I need to stable my horse and grab more firewood in case the power goes out. I've got a feeling we're in for a nasty night. Just rest here with your little puffball and work on warming up, okay?"

After a long moment, she nodded and closed her eyes again.

He knew her somehow and it bothered the hell out

of him that he couldn't place how, especially since he usually prided himself on his ironclad memory.

He watched the dog circle around and then settle on her feet again like a little fuzzy slipper. Whoever she was, she had about as much a sense as that little dog to go out on a night like tonight. Someone was probably worrying about her. After he took care of Tag, he would try to figure out if she needed to call someone with her whereabouts.

Shoving on his Stetson again, he drew in his last breath of warm air for a while and then headed into the teeth of the storm.

He rushed through taking care of Tag and loaded up as much firewood as he could carry in a load toward the house. He had a feeling he would be back and forth to the woodpile several times during the night and he was grateful his tenant/caretaker Gwen Bianca had been conscientious about making sure enough wood was stockpiled for the winter.

What was he going to do without her? He frowned as one more niggling worry pressed in on him.

Ever since she told him she was buying a house closer to Jackson Hole where she frequently showed her pottery, he had been trying to figure out his options. He was a little preoccupied fighting the Taliban to spend much time worrying about whether a woodpile thousands of miles away had been replenished.

When he returned to the house, he checked on his unexpected guest first thing and found her still sleeping. She wasn't shivering anymore and when he touched her forehead, she didn't seem to be running a fever.

The dog barked a little yippy greeting at him but didn't move from her spot at the woman's feet.

He took off his hat and coat and hung them in the mudroom, then returned to the family room. His touching her forehead—or perhaps the dog's bark—must have awakened her. She was sitting up and this time her eyes were finally wide open.

They were a soft and luscious green, the kind of color he dreamed about during the harsh and desolate Afghan winters, of spring grasses covering the mountains, of hope and growth and life.

She gave him a hesitant smile and his jaw sagged as he finally placed how he knew her.

Holy Mother of God.

The woman on his couch, the one he had dressed in his most disreputable sweats, the woman who had crashed her vehicle into Cold Creek just outside his gates and whose little pink panties he had taken such guilty pleasure in glimpsing, was none other than Mimi frigging Van Hoyt.

A man was staring at her.

Not just any man, either. He was tall, perhaps six-one or two, with short dark hair and blue eyes, powerful muscles and a square, determined sort of jaw. He was just the sort of man who made her most nervous, the kind who didn't look as if they could be swayed by a flirty smile and a sidelong look.

He was staring at her as if she had just sprouted horns out of the top of her head. She frowned, uncomfortable with his scrutiny though she couldn't have said exactly why.

Her gaze shifted to her surroundings and she discovered she was on a red plaid sofa in a room she didn't recognize, with rather outdated beige flowered wallpaper and a jumble of mismatched furnishings.

She had no clear memory of arriving here, only a vague sense that something was very wrong in her life, that someone was supposed to help her sort everything out. And then she was driving, driving, with snow flying, and a sharp moment of fear.

She looked at the man again, registering that he was extraordinarily handsome in a clean-cut, all-American sort of way.

Had she been looking for him? She blinked, trying to sort through the jumble of her thoughts.

"How are you feeling?" he finally asked. "I couldn't find any broken bones and I think the air bag probably saved you from a nasty bump on the head when you hit the creek."

Creek. She closed her eyes as a memory returned of her hands gripping a steering wheel and a desperate need to reach someone who could help her.

Baby. The baby.

She clutched her hands over her abdomen and made a low sort of moan.

"Here, take it easy. Do you have a stomachache? That could be from the air bag. It's not unusual to bruise a rib or two when one of those things deploys. Do you want me to take you into the clinic in town to check things out?"

She didn't know. She couldn't think, as if every coherent thought in her head had been squirreled away on a high shelf just out of her reach.

She hugged her arms around herself. She had to trust her instincts, since she didn't know what else to do. "No clinic. I don't want to go to the doctor."

He raised one dark eyebrow at that but then shrugged. "Your call. For now, anyway. If you start babbling and speaking in tongues, I'm calling the doctor in Pine Gulch, no matter what you say."

"Fair enough." The baby was fine, she told herself. She wouldn't accept any other alternative. "Where am I?"

"My ranch. The Western Sky. I told you my name before but I'll do it again. I'm Brant Western."

To her surprise, Simone, who usually distrusted everything with a Y chromosome, jumped down from the sofa to sniff at his boots. He picked the dog up and held her, somehow still managing to look ridiculously masculine with a little powder puff in his arms.

Western Sky. Gwen. *That's* where she had been running. Gwen would fix everything, she knew it.

No. This problem was too big for even Gwen to fix.

"I'm Maura Howard," she answered instinctively, using the alias she preferred when she traveled, for security reasons.

"Are you?" he said. *An odd question,* she thought briefly, but she was more concerned with why she was here and not where she wanted to be.

She had visited Gwen's cabin once before but she didn't remember this room. "This isn't Gwen's house."

At once, a certain understanding flashed in blue eyes that reminded her of the ocean near her beach house in Malibu on her favorite stormy afternoons.

"You know Gwen Bianca?"

She nodded. "I need to call her, to let her know I'm here."

"That's not going to do you much good. Gwen's not around."

That set her back and she frowned. "Do you know where she is?"

"Not at the ranch, I'm afraid. Not even in the country, actually. She's at a gallery opening in Milan."

Oh, no. Mimi closed her eyes. How stupid and short-sighted of her, to assume Gwen would be just waiting here to offer help if Mimi ever needed it.

Egocentric, silly, selfish. That was certainly her.

No wonder she preferred being Maura Howard whenever she had the chance.

"Well, Maura." Was it her imagination, or did he stress her name in an unnatural sort of way? "I'm afraid you're not going anywhere tonight. It's too dangerous for you to drive on these snowy roads even if I could manage to go out in the dark and snow to pull your vehicle out of the creek. I'm afraid you're stuck for now."

Oh, what a mess. She wanted to sink back onto the pillows of this comfortable sofa, just close her eyes and slide back into blissful oblivion. But she couldn't very well do that with her host watching her out of those intense blue eyes.

As tough and dangerous as Brant Western looked, she had the strangest assurance that she was safe with him. On the other hand, her instincts hadn't been all that reliable where men where concerned for the past, oh, twenty-six years.

But Simone liked him and that counted for a great deal in her book.

As if sensing the direction of her gaze, he set the dog down. Simone's white furry face looked crestfallen for just a moment, then she jumped back up to Mimi's lap.

"I'm assuming Gwen didn't know you were coming."

"No. I should have called her." Her voice trembled on the words and she fought down the panic and the fear and the whole tangled mess of emotions she'd been fighting since that stark moment in her ob-gyn's office the day before.

Gwen had been her logical refuge as she faced this latest disaster in her life. Mimi's favorite of her father's ex-wives, Gwen had always offered comfort and support through boarding schools and breakups and scandals.

For twenty-four hours, all she had been able to think about was escaping to Gwen, in desperate need of her calm good sense and her unfailing confidence in Mimi. But Gwen wasn't here. She was in Milan right now, just when Mimi needed her most and she felt, ridiculously, as if all the underpinnings of her world were shaking loose.

First driving her car into a creek and now this. It was all too much. She sniffled and made a valiant effort to fight back the tears, but it was too late. The panic swallowed her whole and she started to cry.

Simone licked at her tears and Mimi held the dog closer, burying her face in her fur.

Through her tears, she thought she saw utter horror in her host's eyes. He was an officer in the military, she remembered Gwen telling her. A major, if Mimi wasn't mistaken, in some Special Forces unit.

She had a vague memory of him telling her that. Major Brant Western, Company A, 1st Battallion, 75th Ranger Regiment.

She would have thought a man would have to be a fairly confident, take-charge sort of guy to reach that rank, but Major Western looked completely panicked by her tears. "Hey, come on. Don't cry, um, Maura. It's okay. You'll see. Things will seem better in the morning, I promise. It's not the end of the world. You're safe and dry now and I've even got a guest room you can stay in tonight. We'll get that cut on your eye cleaned up and bandaged."

She swiped at her tears with her sleeve and a moment later he thrust a tissue in her face, which she seized on gratefully. "I can't stay here," she said after she'd calmed a little. "I don't even know you. I passed a guest ranch a few miles back. Hope Springs or something like that. I'll see if they've got availability."

"How are you going to get there?" he asked.

"What do you mean?"

"Your SUV is toast for now and Pine Gulch isn't exactly flush with cab companies. Beside that, the way that wind is blowing and drifting, it's not safe for anybody to be out on the roads. That storm has already piled up seven inches and forecasters are predicting two or three times that before we're done. I promise, you're completely safe staying here. The guest room's even got a lock on the door."

She had a feeling a locked door wouldn't stop him if he set his mind to breaking in somewhere. No doubt this man, with his serious blue eyes and solid strength, could work his way through just about anything—whether a locked door or a woman's good sense.

"Have you eaten?"

"I'm not hungry."

That was certainly true enough. Just the idea of food made her stomach churn. Ironic that she'd been pregnant for more than ten weeks and hadn't exhibited a single symptom, not the tiniest sign that might have tipped her off. Then the day after she found out she was pregnant, she started with the morning sickness, along with a bone-deep exhaustion. If she had the chance, she thought she could sleep for a week.

"I can't impose on you this way."

He shrugged. "Once you've made a guy wade through a frozen creek twice, what's a little further inconvenience for him? Let me go grab some clean sheets for the bed and we'll get that cut cleaned up and you settled for the night."

She wiped at the tears drying on her features. What choice did she have? She had nowhere else to go. After he left the room, she leaned into the sofa, holding Simone close and soaking in the fire's delicious heat.

Now that she thought of it, this just might be the perfect solution, at least while she tried to wrap her head around the terrifying future.

No one would know where she was. Not her father—as if he'd care. Not Marco, who would care even less. Certainly not the bane of her existence, the paparazzi, who cared only for ratings and circulation numbers.

The world outside that window was a terrifying place. For now she had shelter from that storm out there, and a man who looked more than capable of protecting her from anything that might come along.

She only needed a little breathing space to figure things out and she could find that here as easily as anywhere else.

Only one possible complication occurred to her. She would have to do her best to keep him from calling for a tow when the snow cleared. She knew from experience that people like tow-truck drivers and gas station attendants and restaurant servers were usually the first ones to pick up a phone and call in the tabloids.

She could see the headlines now. Mimi's Ditchscapade with Sexy Rancher.

She couldn't afford that right now. She only needed

a few days of quiet and rest. Like that blizzard out there, the media storm that was her life and this latest—and worst—potential scandal would hopefully pass without ever seeing the light of day.

She only needed to figure out a way to stay safe and warm until it did.

Chapter Two

When Brant returned to his living room, he found Maura Howard—aka Mimi Van Hoyt, tabloid princess du jour—gazing into the fire, her features pale and her wide, mobile mouth set into a tense frown.

A few years ago during one of his Iraq deployments, he'd had the misfortune of seeing her one miserable attempt at moviemaking at a showing in the rec hall in Tikrit. He was pretty sure the apparent turmoil she was showing now must be genuine, since her acting skills had been roughly on par with the howler monkey that had enjoyed a bit in the movie.

As long as she didn't cry again, he could handle things. He was ashamed to admit that he could handle a dozen armed insurgents better than a crying woman.

"Everything will seem better in the morning," he promised her. "Once the storm passes over, I can call a tow for your car. I'm sure they can fix it right up in town and send you on your way."

Her hands twisted on her lap and those deep green eyes shifted away from him. In pictures he'd seen of her, he always thought those eyes held a hard, cynical edge, but he could see none of that here.

"I, um, can't really afford a tow right now."

If she hadn't said the words with such a valiant attempt at sincerity in her voice, he would have snorted outright at that blatant whopper. Everybody on the planet who had ever seen a tabloid knew her father was Werner Van Hoyt, real estate mogul, Hollywood producer and megabillionaire. She was a trust fund baby whose sole existence seemed to revolve around attending the hottest parties and being seen with other quasi-celebrities at the hippest clubs until all hours of the day and night.

Did she think he was a complete idiot? The SUV in question was a Mercedes, for heaven's sake.

But if Mimi wanted to pretend to be someone else, who was he to stop her?

"The rental car company should take care of the details. They would probably even send another vehicle for you. Barring that, I'm sure Wylie down at the garage will take a credit card or work out a payment plan with you. But we can cross that bridge once the snow clears. Let's get your face cleaned up so you can get to bed."

She didn't look as if she appreciated any of those options, at least judging by the frustration tightening her features. He had a pretty strong feeling she probably hadn't been thwarted much in her life. It would probably do her a world of good not to get her way once in a while.

He had to bite his lip to keep from smiling. Big

shocker there. He hadn't found much of anything amusing since that miserable afternoon three weeks ago in a remote village in Paktika Province.

Longer, come to think of it. His world had felt hollow and dark around the edges since Jo's death in the fall. But somehow Mimi seemed to remind him that life could sometimes be a real kick in the seat.

He had to give her credit for only flinching a little when he cleansed the small cut over her eye and stuck a bandage on it.

"It's a pretty small cut and shouldn't leave a scar."

"Thank you," she said in a subdued voice, then gracefully covered a yawn. "I'm sorry. I've been traveling for several hours and it's been a…stressful day."

"Don't worry about it. Your room is back here. It's nothing fancy but it's comfortable and you've got your own bathroom."

"I hate to ask but, speaking of bathrooms," she said, "Simone could probably use a trip outside."

"Yeah, she has been dancing around for the door for the last few minutes. I'll take her out and try to make sure she doesn't get swallowed by the snow, then bring her in to you."

"Thank you for…everything," she murmured. "Not too many people would take in a complete stranger— and her little dog, too—in the middle of a blizzard."

"Maybe not where you're from. But I would guess just about anybody in Cold Creek Canyon would have done the same."

"Then it must be a lovely place."

"Except in the middle of a February blizzard," he answered. She didn't object when he cupped her elbow to help her down the hall and he tried to store up all the memories. How she smelled of some light citrus-floral, undoubtedly expensive perfume. How her silk turtle-neck caressed his fingers. How she was much shorter than he would have guessed, only just reaching his shoulder.

The guys would want to know everything about this surreal interlude and Brant owed it to them to memorize every single detail.

Like the rest of the house, the guest suite was on the shabby side, with aging furniture and peeling wallpaper. But it had a comfortable queen-sized bed, an electric fireplace he'd turned on when he made up the bed and a huge claw-foot tub in the bathroom.

The main house had been mostly empty for the past two years except for his occasional visits between deployments. Since he left Cold Creek a dozen years ago for the military, he had rented the house out sporadically. Gwen Bianca stayed in the small cabin on the property rent-free in exchange for things like keeping the woodpile stocked and the roof from collapsing in.

His last tenants had moved out six months ago and he hadn't bothered to replace them since the rent mostly covered barebones maintenance and county property taxes on the land anyway and was hardly worth the trouble most of the time.

Now that Gwen had announced she was moving away, he didn't know what to do with Western Sky.

"It's not much but you should be warm and comfortable."

"I'll be fine. Thank you again for your hospitality."

"I don't know if this is a warning or an apology in advance, but I'll be checking on you occasionally in the night."

"Do you think I'm going to run off with your plasma TV?"

He fought another smile, wondering where they were all coming from. "You're welcome to it, if you think you can make a clean getaway on foot in this storm. No. There's a chance you had a head injury. I don't think so but you were in and out of consciousness for a while there. I can't take any chance of missing signs of swelling or unusual behavior."

She sat on the edge of the bed with a startled sort of work. "I appreciate your...diligence, but I'm sure I don't have a brain injury. The air bag protected me."

"I guess you forgot to mention you were a neurologist."

She frowned. "I'm not."

"What are you, then?" he asked, curious as to how she would answer. Heiress? Aimless socialite? Lousy actress?

After a long pause, she forced a smile. "I work for a charitable organization in Los Angeles."

Nice save, he thought. It could very well be true, since she had enough money to rescue half the world.

"Well, unless your charitable organization specializes in self-diagnosing traumatic brain injuries, I'm going to have to err on the side of caution here and stick to the plan of checking on you through the night."

"Don't tell me you're the neurologist now."

"Nope. Just an Army Ranger who's been hit over the head a few too many times in my career. I'll check on you about every hour to make sure your mental status hasn't changed."

"How would you even know if my mental status has changed or not? You just met me."

He laughed out loud at that, a rusty sound that surprised the heck out of him.

"True enough. I guess when you stand on your head and start reciting the Declaration of Independence at four in the morning, I'll be sure to ask if that's normal behavior before I call the doctor."

She almost smiled in return but he sensed she was troubled about more than just her car accident.

None of his concern, he reminded himself. Whatever she was doing in this isolated part of Idaho was her own business.

"I put one of my T-shirts on the bed there for you to sleep in. I'll bring your little purse pooch back after I let her out. Let me know if you need anything else or if you get hungry. The Western Sky isn't a four-star resort but I can probably rustle up some tea and toast."

"Right now I only want to rest."

"Can't blame you there," he answered. "It's been a strange evening all the way around. Come on, pup."

The little dog barked, her black eyes glowing with eagerness in her white fur, and followed him into the hallway.

The wind still howled outside but he managed to find a spot of ground somewhat sheltered by the back patio awning for her to delicately take care of business.

To his relief, the dog didn't seem any more inclined to stay out in the howling storm than he did. She hurried back to where he stood on the steps and he scooped her up and carried her inside, where he dried off her paws with an old towel.

He refused to admit to himself that he was trying to spare Mimi four cold, wet paws against her when the dog jumped up on her bed.

When he softly knocked on the guest room door, she didn't answer. After a moment, he took the liberty of pushing it open. She was already asleep, her eyes closed, and he set the dog beside her on the bed, thinking she would need the comfort of the familiar if she awoke in a strange place in the middle of the night.

From the dim light in the hallway, he could just make out her high cheekbones and that lush, kissable mouth.

She was even prettier in person, just about the loveliest thing he had ever seen in real life.

She was beautiful and she made him forget the ghosts that haunted him, even if only for a little while. For a guy who only had a week before he had to report back to a war zone, both of those things seemed pretty darn seductive right about now.

Not the most restful sleep she had ever experienced.

At 6:00 a.m., after a night of being awakened several times by the keening wind outside and by her unwilling host insistent on checking her questionable mental status, she awoke to Simone licking her face.

Mimi groaned as her return to consciousness brought with it assorted aches and pains. The sting of the cut on her forehead and the low throb of a headache at the base of her skull were the worst of them. Her shoulder muscles ached, but she had a feeling that was more from the stress of the past two days than from any obvious injury.

She pushed away her assorted complaints to focus on the tiny bichon frise she adored. "Do you need to go outside, sweetie?" she asked.

Instead of leaping from the bed and scampering to the door as she normally would have done, Simone merely yawned, stretched her four paws out, then closed her eyes again.

"I guess not," Mimi answered with a frown at that bit of unusual behavior. Simone usually jumped to go outside first thing after a full night of holding her bladder. Mimi could only hope she hadn't decided to relieve herself somewhere in this strange house.

She looked around the bedroom in the pale light of predawn but couldn't see any obvious signs of a mishap in any corner. What she *did* find was her entire set of luggage piled up inside the door, all five pieces of it, including Simone's carrier.

The sight of them all stunned her and sent a funny little sparkle jumping through her. Somehow in the middle of the raging blizzard, Major Western had gone to the trouble of retrieving every one of them for her.

In the night, more vague recollections had come together in her head and she vividly remembered he had been forced to wade through the ice-crusted creek to reach her after the accident. In order to retrieve her luggage from the SUV, he would have had to venture into that water yet again. She could hardly believe he had done that for her, yet the proof was right there before her eyes in the corner.

No. There had to be some catch. He just seemed entirely too good to be real. The cynical part of her that had been burned by men a few dozen too many times couldn't quite believe anyone would find her worth that much effort.

She pressed a hand to her stomach, to the tiny secret growing there.

"Are you okay in there, kiddo?" she murmured.

She had bought a half-dozen pregnancy books the moment she left the doctor's office but hadn't dared read any of them on the plane, afraid to risk that someone would see through her disguise and tip off the tabloids about her reading choices. Instead, she'd had to be content with a pregnancy week-by-week app on her cell phone, and she had devoured every single word behind her sunglasses on the plane.

At barely eleven weeks, Mimi knew she wasn't far enough along to actually feel the baby move. Maybe in a few more weeks. But that didn't stop her from imagining the little thing swimming around in there.

Something else that didn't feel quite real to her, that in a few months she was going to be a mother. She had only had two days to absorb the stunning news that her brief but intense affair with Marco Mendez had resulted in an unexpected complication.

In only a few days, the provider of half her baby's DNA was marrying another woman. And not just any woman but Jessalyn St. Claire, Hollywood's current favorite leading lady, sweet and cute and universally adored. Marco and Jessalyn. "Messalyn," as the tabloids dubbed the pair of them. The two beautiful, talented, successful people were apparently enamored of each other.

It was a match made in heaven—or their respective publicists' offices. Mimi wasn't sure which.

She only knew that if word leaked out that she was expecting Marco Mendez's baby, Jessalyn would flip out, especially since the timing of Mimi's pregnancy would clearly reveal that they had carried on their affair several months after Marco had proposed to Jessalyn in such a public venue as the Grammy Awards, where he won Best Male Vocalist of the year.

Mimi probed her heart for the devastation she probably should be feeling right about now. For two months, she had been expecting Marco to break off the sham engagement and publicly declare he loved Mimi, as he had privately assured her over and over was his intention.

The declaration never came. She felt like an idiot for ever imagining it would. Worse, when she had gathered up every bit of her courage and whatever vestiges of pride she had left and finally called him to meet her at their secret place after the stunning discovery of her pregnancy, he hadn't reacted at all like she had stupidly hoped.

Arrogant, egocentric, selfish.

She was all those things and more. She had secretly hoped that when Marco found out she was pregnant, he would pull her into his arms and declare he couldn't go through with the marriage now, that he loved her and wanted to spend the rest of his life with her and the child they had created.

She was pathetically stupid.

Instead, his sleek, sexy features had turned bone-white and he had asked her if she'd made an appointment yet to take care of the problem.

When she hesitantly told him she was thinking about keeping the baby, he had become enraged. She had never believed Marco capable of violence until he had stood with veins popping out in his neck, practically foaming at the mouth in that exclusive, secluded house in Topanga Canyon he kept for these little trysts.

He had called her every vile name in the book and some she'd never heard of. By the time he was done, she felt like all those things he called her. Skank. Whore. Bitch.

And worse.

In the end, she'd somehow found the strength to tell him emphatically that keeping the baby or not would be her own decision. If she kept the baby, it would be hers alone and he would relinquish any claim to it. She wanted nothing more to do with him.

If he touched her or threatened her again in any way, she would tell her father, a man both of them knew had the power to decimate careers before he'd taken a sip of his morning soy latte.

She pressed a hand to her tiny baby bump.

"I'm sorry I picked such a jerk to be your daddy," she whispered.

She loved this baby already. The idea of it, innocent and sweet, seemed to wrap around all the empty places in her heart. The only blessing in the whole mess was that she and Marco had, unbelievably, been able to keep their affair a secret thus far.

Oh, maybe a few rumors had been circulating here and there. But she figured if she stayed out of the camera glare at least until the wedding was over and then took an extended trip somewhere quiet, she just might muddle through this whole thing. She had no doubt she could find someone willing to claim paternity for enough money.

Or maybe she would just drop out of sight for the rest of her life, relocate to some isolated place in the world where people had never heard of Mimi Van Hoyt or her more ridiculous antics.

Borneo might be nice. Or she could move in with some friendly indigenous tribe along the Amazon.

Staying with Gwen at least until the wedding was over would have solved her short-term problem, if she hadn't been too blasted shortsighted to pick up the phone first.

Why couldn't she still stay here?

The thought was undeniably enticing. Gwen might not be here but, except for her absence, the ranch still offered all the advantages that had led Mimi to fly out on a snowy February afternoon to find her ex-stepmother. It was isolated and remote, as far from the craziness of a celebrity wedding as Mimi could imagine.

She thought of her host wading through a creek in the middle of a blizzard to retrieve her luggage. He seemed a decent sort of man, with perhaps a bit of a hero complex. Maybe Major Western could be convinced to let her stay just for a few days.

She closed her eyes, daunted by the very idea of asking him. Though she had never had much trouble bending the males of the species to her will—her father being the most glaring exception—she had a feeling Brant Western wouldn't be such an easy sell.

Later. She would wait until the sun was at least up before she worried about it, she decided with a yawn.

When she awoke again, a muted kind of daylight streamed through the curtains and an entirely too male figure was standing beside her bed.

"Morning." Her voice came out sultry and low, more a product of sleepiness than any effort to be sexy, but something flared in his eyes for just a moment, then was gone.

Okay, maybe convincing him she should stay wouldn't be as difficult as she had feared, Mimi thought, hiding a secret smile even as she was a little disappointed he wouldn't present more of a challenge.

"Good morning." His voice was a little more tightly wound than she remembered and she thought his eyes looked tired. From monitoring her all night? she wondered. Or from something else?

"Sorry to wake you but I haven't been in to check on

you for a couple of hours. I was just seeing if the dog needed to go out again."

"Did you take her out in the night?"

He nodded. "She's not too crazy about snow."

"Oh, I know. Once in Chamonix she got lost in a snow drift. It was terrifying for both of us."

She shouldn't have said that, she realized at once. Maura Howard wasn't the sort to visit exclusive ski resorts in the Swiss Alps, but Brant didn't seem to blink an eye.

"I'm on my way to take care of the horses. I'll put her out again before I leave and I'll try not to lose her in the snow. How's your head?"

"Better. The rest of me is a little achy but I'll survive. Is it still storming?"

He nodded tersely as she sat up in bed and seemed intent on keeping his gaze fixed on some fixed spot in the distance as if he were standing at attention on parade somewhere. "We've had more than a foot and it's still coming down." He paused. "There's a good chance you might be stuck here another day or two. It's going to take at least that long for the plows to clear us out."

"Oh, no!"

Though secretly relieved, she figured he expected the news to come as a shock, so she tried to employ her glaringly nonexistent acting skills. Then, pouring it on a little thicker, she stretched a little before tucking a wayward curl behind her ear.

She didn't miss the way his pupils flared just a little, even as he pretended not to pay her any attention.

"I'm so sorry to be even more of an inconvenience to you, Major Western."

"Around here I'm plain Brant."

"Brant." It was a strong, masculine name that somehow fit him perfectly.

"Thank you so much for bringing my luggage in. It was so kind of you."

"No big deal. I thought you would feel more comfortable if you had your own things, especially since it looks like you're going to be here another night."

"I feel so foolish. If I'd only called Gwen before showing up on her doorstep like this, you wouldn't be stuck with me now."

"That was a pretty idiotic thing to do," he agreed flatly. "What would have happened to you if you'd slid off in a spot in the canyon that wasn't so close to any houses? You might have been stuck in the storm in your car all night and probably would have frozen to death before anybody found you."

His bluntness grated and she almost glared but at the last minute she remembered she needed his help. Or maybe not. She needed a place to stay, but that didn't necessarily mean she had to stay with *him*.

"I hate imposing on you," she said as another idea suddenly occurred to her, one she couldn't believe she hadn't thought of the night before or this morning when she was mulling over her various options. "What if we called Gwen and asked her if I could stay at her house since she's gone?"

"Great idea," he said, with somewhat humiliating alacrity. "There's only one problem with it. Gwen's furnace went out the day she left. I've got a company coming out to replace it but they can't make it to the ranch until later in the week. With the blizzard, it might even be next week before they come out. Occupied dwellings have precedence in weather like this so I'm afraid you're stuck here until the storm clears."

She tried to look appropriately upset by that news. At least his insistence on that particular point would give her a little breathing room to figure out how she could convince him to let her stay longer.

Four hours later, she was rethinking her entire strategy.

If she had to stay here until Marco's wedding was over, she was very much afraid she would die of boredom.

She had never been very good with dead time. She liked to fill it with friends and shopping and trips to her favorite day spa. Okay, she had spent twenty-six years wading in shallow waters. She had no problem admitting it. She liked having fun and wasn't very good at finding ways to entertain herself.

That particular task seemed especially challenging here at Western Sky. Major Western had very few books—most were in storage near his home base in Georgia, he had told her—and the DVD selection was limited. And of course the satellite television wasn't working because too much snow had collected in the dish, blocking the receiver. Or at least that's the explanation her host provided.

The house wasn't wired to the Internet, since he was rarely here and didn't use it much anyway.

She probably could have dashed off some texts and even an e-mail or two on her Smartphone, but she had made the conscious decision to turn it off. For now, she was Maura Howard. It might be a little tough selling that particular story if she had too much contact with the outside world.

Her host had made himself scarce most of the day,

busy looking over ranch accounts or bringing in fire-wood or knocking ice out of the water troughs for the livestock.

She had a feeling he was avoiding her, though she wasn't sure why, which left her with Simone for company.

Brant poked his head into the kitchen just after noon to tell her to help herself to whatever she wanted for lunch but that he had a bit of a crisis at Gwen's cabin with frozen pipes since the furnace wasn't working.

Mimi had settled on a solitary lunch of canned tomato soup that was actually quite tasty. After she washed and dried her bowl, marveling that there was a house in America which actually didn't possess a dishwasher, she returned it to the rather dingy cupboard next to the sink and was suddenly hit by a brainstorm.

This was how she could convince Brant to let her stay.

A brilliant idea, if she did say so herself. Not bad for a shallow girl, she thought some time later as she surveyed the contents of every kitchen cupboard, jumbled on all the countertops.

She stood on a stepladder with a bucket of sudsy water in front of her as she scoured years of grease and dust from the top of his knotty pine cabinets.

Here was a little known secret the tabloids had never unearthed about Mimi Van Hoyt. They would probably have a field day if anyone ever discovered she liked to houseclean when she was bored or stressed.

Between boarding school stays, her father's long-term housekeeper Gert used to give her little chores to do. Cleaning out a closet, organizing a drawer, polishing silver. Her father probably never would have allowed it if he'd known, but she and Gert had both been very good at keeping secrets from Werner Van Hoyt.

She had never understood why she enjoyed it so much and always been a little ashamed of what she considered a secret vice until one of her more insightful therapists had pointed out those hours spent with Gert at some mundane task or other were among the most consistent of her life. Perhaps cleaning her surroundings was her mental way of creating order out of the chaos that was her life amid her father's multiple marriages and divorces.

Here in Major Western's house, it was simply something to pass the time, she told herself, digging in a little harder on a particularly tough stain.

"What would you be doing?"

Mimi jerked her head around and found Major Western standing in the kitchen doorway watching her with an expression that seemed a complicated mix— somewhere between astonished and appalled.

Simone—exceptional watchdog that she was— awoke at his voice and jumped up from her spot on a half-circle rug by the sink. She yipped an eager greeting while Mimi flushed to the roots of her hair.

"Sorry. I was…bored."

He gave her a skeptical look. "Bored. And so, out of the blue, you decided to wash out my kitchen cabinets."

"Somebody needed to. You wouldn't believe the grime on them."

She winced as soon as the words escaped. Okay, that might not be the most tactful thing to mention to a man she was hoping would keep her around for a few days.

"You've been busy with your Army career, I'm sure," she quickly amended. "I can only imagine how difficult it is to keep a place like this clean when you're not here all the time."

He looked both rueful and embarrassed as he moved farther into the kitchen and started taking off his winter gear.

"I've been renting it out on and off for the last few years and tenants don't exactly keep the place in the best shape. I'm planning on having a crew come in after I return to Afghanistan to clean it all out and whip it into shape before I put it on the market."

She paused her scrubbing, struck both that he had been in Afghanistan and that he would put such a wonderful house on the market. "Why would you sell this place? I can't see much out there except snow right now but I would guess it's a beautiful view. At least Gwen always raves about what inspiration she finds here for her work."

He unbuttoned his soaked coat and she tried not to notice the muscles of his chest that moved under his sweater as he worked his arms out of the sleeves.

"It's long past time."

He was quiet for several moments. "The reality is, I'm only here a few weeks of the year, if that, and it's too hard to take care of the place long-distance, even with your friend Gwen keeping an eye on things for me. Anyway, Gwen's leaving, too. She told me she's buying a house outside Jackson Hole and that just seemed the final straw. I can't even contemplate how daunting it would be to find someone to replace her. Not to mention keeping up with general maintenance like painting the barn."

It was entirely too choice an opportunity to pass up. "This is perfect. I'll help you."

Again that eyebrow crept up as he toed off his winter

boots. "You want to paint the barn? I'm afraid that might be a little tough, what with the snow and all."

She frowned. "Not the barn. But this." She pointed with her soapy towel. "The whole place needs a good scrubbing, as I'm sure you're aware."

He stared at her. "Let me get this straight. You're volunteering to clean my house?"

She set the soapy towel back in the bucket and perched on the top rung of the ladder to face him. "Sure, why not?"

"I can think of a few pretty compelling reasons."

She flashed him a quick look, wondering what he meant by that, but she couldn't read anything in his expression.

"The truth is, I need a place to stay for a few days."

"Why?"

"It's a long, boring story."

"Somehow I doubt that," he murmured, looking fascinated.

"Trust me," she said firmly. "I need a place to stay for a few days—let's just leave it at that—and you could use some work done around here to help you ready the place for prospective buyers."

"And you think you can help me do that?"

The skepticism in his voice stung, for reasons she didn't want to examine too carefully. "Believe it or not, I've actually helped a friend stage houses for sale before and I know a little about it. I can help you, I swear. Why shouldn't we both get something we need?"

He leaned against the counter next to the refrigerator and crossed his arms over his chest. As he studied her, she thought she saw doubt, lingering shock and an odd sort of speculation in his eyes.

After a moment he shook his head. "I can't ask you to do that, Ms. Howard."

"You didn't ask. I'm offering."

Five days. That was all she needed to avoid Hollywood's biggest wedding in years. With a little time and distance, she hoped she could figure out what she was going to do with the mess of her life.

"I really do need a place to stay, Major Western."

She thought she saw a softening in the implacable set to his jaw, a tiny waver in his eyes, so she whipped out the big guns. The undefeated, never-fail, invincible option.

She beamed at him, her full-throttle, pour-on-the-charm smile that had made babbling fools out of every male she'd ever wielded it on. "I swear, you'll be so happy with the job I do, you might just decide not to sell."

Though she saw obvious reluctance in his dark eyes, he finally sighed. "A few days. Why not? As long as you don't make any major changes. Just clean things out a little and make the rooms look better. That's all."

Relief coursed through her. Simone, sensing Mimi's excitement, barked happily.

"You won't regret it, I promise."

He shook his head and reached into the refrigerator for a bottled water. In his open, honest expression, she could see he was already sorry. She didn't care, she told herself, ignoring that same little sting under her heart. Whether he wanted her here or not, somehow she knew that Major Brant Western was too honorable to kick her out after he'd promised she could stay.

Chapter Three

What kind of game was she playing?

That seemed to be the common refrain echoing through his brain when it came to Mimi Van Hoyt. He still hadn't come any closer to figuring her out several hours after their stunning conversation, as they sat at the worn kitchen table eating a cobbled-together dinner of canned stew and peaches.

First she was pretending to be someone else—as if anyone in the world with access to a computer or a television could somehow have been lucky enough to miss her many well-publicized antics. The woman couldn't pick up her newspaper in the morning without a crop of photographers there to chronicle every move and she must think he was either blind or stupid not to figure out who she was.

But that same tabloid darling who apparently didn't

step outside her door without wearing designer clothes had spent the afternoon cleaning every nook and cranny of his kitchen—and doing a pretty good job of it. Not that he was any great judge of cleanliness, having spent most of his adult life on Army bases or in primitive conditions in the field, but he had grown up with Jo Winder as an example and he knew she would have been happy to see the countertops sparkling and the old wood cabinets gleaming with polish.

He wouldn't have believed it if he hadn't seen it himself—Mimi Van Hoyt, lush and elegant, scrubbing the grime away from a worn-out ranch house with no small degree of relish. She seemed as happy with her hands in a bucket of soapy water as he was out on patrol with his M4 in his hands.

She had even sung a little under her breath, for heaven's sake, and he couldn't help wondering why she had dabbled in acting instead of singing since her contralto voice didn't sound half-bad.

That low, throaty voice seemed to slide down his spine like trailing fingers and a few times he'd had to manufacture some obvious excuse to leave the house just to get away from it. He figured he'd hauled enough wood up to the house to last them all week but he couldn't seem to resist returning to the kitchen to watch her.

The woman completely baffled him. He would have expected her to be whining about the lack of entertainment in the cabin, about the enforced confinement, about the endless snow.

At the very least, he would have thought her fingers would be tapping away at some cell phone as she tweeted or whatever it was called, about being trapped in an isolated Idaho ranch with a taciturn stranger.

Instead, she teased her little dog, she took down his curtains and threw them in the washing machine, she organized every ancient cookbook left in the cupboard.

She seemed relentlessly cheerful while the storm continued to bluster outside.

Somehow he was going to have to figure out a way to snap her picture when she wasn't looking. Otherwise, his men would never believe he'd spent his mid-tour leave watching Mimi Van Hoyt scrub grease off his stove vent.

But he was pretty sure a photograph wouldn't show them how lovely she looked, with those huge, deep green eyes and her long inky curls and that bright smile that took over her entire face.

Though he knew it was dangerous, Brant couldn't seem to stop watching her. Having Mimi Van Hoyt flitting around his kitchen in all her splendor was a little overwhelming for a man who hadn't been with a woman in longer than he cared to remember—sort of like shoving a starving man in front of one of those all-you-can-eat buffets in Las Vegas and ordering him to dig in.

He'd had an on-again, off-again relationship with a nurse at one of the field support hospitals in Paktika Province, but his constant deployments hadn't left him much time for anything serious.

Not that he was looking. He would leave that sort of thing to the guys who were good at it, like Quinn seemed to be, though he never would have believed it.

Brant treated the women he dated with great respect but he knew he tended to gravitate toward smart, focused career women who weren't looking for anything more than a little fun and companionship once in a while.

Mimi was something else entirely. He didn't know exactly what, but he couldn't believe he had agreed to let her stay at his ranch for a few days. Hour upon hour of trying to ignore the way her hair just begged to be released from the elastic band holding it back or the way those big green eyes caught the light or how her tight little figure danced around the kitchen as she worked.

He shook his head. Which of the two of them was crazier? Right now, he was willing to say it was a toss-up, though he had a suspicion he just might be edging ahead.

"Would you like more stew?" she asked, as if she were hosting some fancy dinner party instead of dishing up canned Dinty Moore.

"I'm good. Thanks."

Though he knew she had to be accustomed to much fancier meals, she did a credible job with her own bowl of stew. He supposed all that scrubbing and dusting must have worked up an appetite.

"Have you had the ranch for long?" she asked, breaking what had been a comfortable silence. "I'm sorry, I can't remember what you told me the name was."

"The Western Sky. And yeah, it's been in my family for generations. My great-great-grandfather bought the land and built the house in the late 1800s."

"So you were raised here?"

He thought of his miserable childhood and the pain and insecurity of it, and then of the Winders, who had rescued him from it and showed him what home could really be.

Explaining all that to her would be entirely too complicated, even if he were willing to discuss it, so he took the easy way out. "For the most part," he answered, hoping she would leave it at that.

Because he was intensely curious to see how far she would take her alternate identity, he turned the conversation back in her direction. "What about you, Maura? Whereabouts do you call home?"

The vibrant green of her eyes seemed to dim a little and she looked away. "Oh, you know. Here and there. California. For now."

"Oh? Which part of the state, if you don't mind me asking?"

"Southern. The L.A. area."

He didn't really follow entertainment gossip but he thought he read or heard something once about her having two homes not far from each other, one her father's Bel Air estate and the other a Malibu beachhouse.

"Is that where your parents live?"

Her mouth tightened a little and she moved the remaining chunks of stew around in her bowl. "My mom died when I was three, just after my parents divorced. My dad sort of raised me but he…we… moved around a lot."

He had to take a quick sip of soda to keep from snorting at that evasive comment—probably Mimi's way of saying her father had residences across the globe.

"And you said you work for a charitable foundation?"

Her wide, mobile mouth pursed into a frown. "Yes. But you probably wouldn't have heard of it."

"And what sort of things do you do there?" He wasn't sure why he enjoyed baiting her so much but it was the most fun he'd had in a long time.

If nothing else, her presence distracted him from the grim events he had left behind in Afghanistan.

"Oh, you know. This and that. I help with fundraising and…and event planning. That sort of thing."

"I don't see a ring, so I'm assuming you're not married."

If he remembered right, she'd been engaged a few years ago to some minor European royalty but he couldn't remember details, other than he thought the breakup had been messy and had, of course, involved some sort of scandal.

"No. Never. You?"

"Nope. Did you ever tell me how you knew Gwen?"

That, at least, was genuine curiosity and not baiting, since his artistic, eclectic, reclusive tenant didn't seem the sort to hobnob with debutantes.

"She was…friends with my father. Years ago. We've always stayed in touch."

Now *that* was interesting. Apparently Gwen Bianca had a few secrets she'd never divulged in the eight or so years she'd been living at the ranch. A past relationship with Werner Van Hoyt? He would never have suspected.

Mimi finally seemed to tire of his subtle interrogation and while he was still digesting the surprising insight into Gwen, she turned the tables on him.

"So how could you possibly want to sell a piece of beautiful land that's been in your family for generations?"

He shrugged. "I don't know if it's fair to say I *want* to sell."

"So don't. The house might be a little worse for wear but it's not falling down around your ears."

"Not yet, anyway."

"A few more years and you'll be retiring from the military, won't you? You'll need a place to settle then, right?"

He had always planned exactly that. But after a half-dozen close calls in his deployment, he'd come to accept that he probably wouldn't live long enough to retire. He didn't have a death wish by any means but he was also a realist.

Since the ambush a month ago, he'd also begun to formulate another motive, one he didn't feel like sharing with a flighty celebrity who spent more on a pair of shoes than some of his men made in a month of hard combat.

"You don't have any other family who might want to do something with the ranch to keep it in the family?" she pressed.

"No. Just me. I...had a younger brother but he died when we were kids."

As soon as he heard his own words, he wanted to take them back. He never spoke about Curtis or his death. Never.

The twenty-year-old guilt might be an integral piece of him, as much a part of the whole as his blue eyes and the crescent-shaped birthmark on his shoulder, but it was private and personal.

"I'm sorry," she murmured, her eyes mossy green with a compassion he didn't want to see. "What happened?"

He wanted to tell her to mind her own business, but since he had been the one to open that particular doorway into the past, he couldn't very well slam it in her face. "He drowned in the creek when I was eleven and he was nine," he finally said.

"The same creek I crashed into?"

He nodded. "There's not much to it now and it might be a little hard to believe, but it's a far different beast in late spring and early summer during the runoff. You know how your SUV went down a slope about five or six feet? During the runoff, that's all full of fast-moving water. So we were being kids and throwing rocks in the creek, even though we weren't supposed to play around it in the springtime. Curtis got a little too close and the bank gave way. I ran downstream and tried to go in after him but…he slipped past me and I couldn't grab him."

"You could have been killed!"

He should have been. That's what his mother had said once in the middle of a bender. *Better you than my sweet baby,* she had said in that emotionless voice that seemed all the more devastating. He wanted to think she hadn't meant it. Curtis had been the funny, smart, adorable one, while Brant had been big and awkward, far too serious for a kid.

After Curtis's death, what had been a tense home life degenerated to sheer misery. The ranch was falling into chaos, his parents fought all the time and both drank heavily. The fighting and the yelling had been one thing. Then his mother had left them and his father had turned all his anger and grief and bitterness against Brant.

That life might have continued indefinitely until one of two things happened—either he grew large enough to pound back or until the old man killed him. He didn't know which would have happened first because Guff and Jo Winder had stepped in.

He sipped at his soda pop, remembering the events that had changed his life. He had felt the Winders' scrutiny a few times when he'd been in town with his father and once Guff had even said something to J.D. when his father climbed up his grill about something or other at the farm implement store, but his intervention had only earned Brant a harsher beating when they got home.

Then one day Guff had stopped at the Western Sky to pick up a couple of weaned calves and his visit just happened to coincide with one of J.D.'s bad drunks. Brant had tried to hide the bruises but his T-shirt had ridden up when he'd been helping load one of the calves into the Winder stock trailer.

Guff had taken one look at the welts crisscrossing his back and Brant would never forget the instant fury in his gaze. He had been conditioned over the years to shrink from that kind of anger, but instead of coming after him, Guff had picked up a pitchfork and backed J.D. against the wall.

"You son of a bitch," he had said in a low, terrible voice. "You've lost one son through a terrible accident. How are you going to live with yourself if you lose the other one at your own hand?"

J.D. had blustered and yelled but Guff had kept that pitchfork on him while he turned to Brant. "You know me and my wife, Jo, have taken in a relative, a boy about your age. I think he goes to school with you. Quinn Southerland. We've got plenty of room at Winder Ranch and I swear on the soul of your brother that no one there will ever lift a hand to you. Would you like to come stay with us for a while?"

He had been as dazed and shocked as his father. Part of him had desperately wanted to leave the Western Sky, to get as far away as he could. But even then, he'd known his duty.

"I'd best stay with my dad, sir. He's got no one else."

Guff had studied him for a long moment, tears in his eyes, then he had dropped the pitchfork. While his dad slid down the wall of the barn to sit in a dazed stupor, Guff had hugged Brant hard and he had realized in that moment that it had been two long years since he'd been touched with anything but malice.

"You're a good boy, son," Guff had said. "I know you love your dad, but right now you have to protect him and yourself. If I promise to see your dad gets the help he needs, will you come?"

In the end, he had agreed, though it had been the toughest choice of his young life, much more difficult than Ranger training or his first combat mission.

He had spent those first few months at Winder Ranch consumed with guilt but certain he would be back with his father at Christmas. True to his word, Guff had paid for his dad's rehab and told J.D. he had to stay sober six months before they would trust him with his son again.

J.D. had lasted only a month before he'd bought a bottle of Jack Daniels, consumed most of it, then wandered into the corral with their meanest bull, where he'd been gored to death.

"I'm sorry."

He jerked his mind from the past to find Mimi watching him across the table with that sympathy in those big green eyes. It took him a moment to register that she was still talking about his brother's death that had changed everything.

"Thanks. So, yeah. In answer to your question, I'm the only one left in my family. And since I've been here a total of maybe three weeks in the last five years, it seems foolish to hang on to the place."

She looked as if she didn't agree, which he found odd. Still, after a moment, she shrugged. "It should sell easily, especially if you clear out some of the clutter and maybe put a few fresh coats of paint in some of the rooms."

"I don't want to put too much energy into the house," he said, finishing off the peaches. "The only ones who can afford this kind of acreage these days are, uh, Hollywood types who will probably tear down the house and build their own in its place. That's what's happened to several nearby ranches."

As he expected, she ignored the Hollywood jab. How could she do otherwise without revealing her true identity? "You never know. The house has a rustic kind of charm and some people are looking for that. With a little effort, you can show off the lovely old bones of the house. A small investment now could help you set a nice asking price for both the house and the land."

He stared at her. "I thought you said you worked for a charitable organization. For a minute there, you sounded like a real estate agent."

Her cheeks turned pink. "No. I just watch a lot of late-night TV infomercials. You know the ones. How to make a fortune in real estate."

"A dream of yours, is it?" he asked in what he hoped was a bland tone. "To make a fortune?"

"Of course," she said with a tiny smile. "Who wouldn't want to have a fortune?"

Though her words were light, he thought he sensed a ribbon of bitterness twining through them. Maybe being a trust fund baby wasn't all parties and private jets.

"Anyway, right now I don't need a fortune," she said, in what he knew was a vast understatement. "Only a place to stay for a few days and something to do while I'm here. I'm grateful you've been kind enough to give me both."

Yeah, he was going to have a hell of a story when this was all over.

* * *

By the next day, Mimi was beginning to think stripping naked and tap-dancing in front of the paparazzi might be easier in the long run than the chore she'd set in front of herself.

She coughed at the cloud of dust that erupted as she yanked down the old-fashioned gingham curtains in the second bedroom upstairs. Simone sneezed, shaking her fuzzy little head. Her formerly pristine little white poochie was now the washed-out, yellow-gray of fading newsprint.

"You are going to need a serious bath," she told the dog ruefully. "Both of us are, I'm afraid."

Simone yipped and continued sniffing around the corners of the room, her tail wagging a mile a minute.

At least her dog was enjoying this little adventure of theirs. Mimi sighed. She wasn't hating it, it was just a bigger task than she had envisioned the day before.

The house wasn't filthy, exactly, just filled with the sort of grime that settled in homes where no one lived. Her father kept full-time staff at each of his residences but even then, dust tended to collect.

After a full day of cleaning and organizing, she was beginning to fear she had taken on a job too big for her to handle. Performing small housekeeping jobs under Gert's supervision in a well-maintained mansion with a large staff was a much different proposition than cleaning out a house that had been largely empty for the past several years.

She felt as grimy as these curtains and she had to wonder what her friends would say if they could see her now, with her hair covered by a particularly ugly Hermès scarf her latest stepmother had given her for Christmas and her skin covered in the same film as the walls.

This had been one of her more harebrained ideas—and that was saying something, since she'd had more than her share.

A few days ago when she flew from L.A. to Jackson Hole, she had expected to find herself being pampered by Gwen, coddled and taken care of by the one person in the world she counted on to care that she was pregnant and frightened and alone.

Instead, here she was dusting out corners and scrubbing baseboards for a man who had hardly said a half-dozen words to her since dinner the night before.

While the storm raged outside after dinner, he had mostly avoided her until she had fallen asleep on the sofa watching a DVD of a romantic comedy she'd seen twice already. He had rather tersely awakened her after nine and suggested she go sleep where she could stretch out.

This morning, he had been awake and out taking care of the horses and checking Gwen's pipes when Mimi awoke, at least according to the brusque note he'd left propped on the kitchen table.

"Help yourself to food," he had instructed, and Mimi had made a face at the note before grabbing a yogurt and a piece of toast.

That was the sum total of her interaction with another human being all day.

She wouldn't feel sorry for herself. That was the old Mimi. The new Mimi was all about finding her own inner strength, taking care of herself. She was twenty-six years old and going to be a mother in six months, responsible for another human being. It was long past time she took that terrifying step into adulthood.

She wadded up the dingy curtains into a bundle in her arms and was just about to carry them downstairs to the washing machine in the mudroom off the kitchen when she heard the front door open.

"Hey, Brant?" a distinctively feminine voice called out. "You know you've got a Mercedes stuck in your creek?"

Oh, crap. Mimi's arms tightened on the curtains. Despite her best efforts at avoiding the outside world, she supposed it was inevitable that Brant might have a visitor.

Her heart pounded as she backed against the wall, out of sight from the foot of the stairs. What should she do? Hide up here and hope whoever it was just went away? Or take her chances that she could bluff her way through and Brant's visitor wouldn't drive away from the Western Sky and immediately call TMZ?

A moment later, Simone took the choice out of her hands. Before Mimi could even think to stop her, the little dog bulleted out of the bedroom and scampered down the stairs, yipping the whole way.

"Well, hello," Mimi heard the woman say in surprise to the dog. "Where did you come from? Brant? What's going on? Whose car and whose dog?"

Mimi drew in a deep breath, dropped the curtains into a heap and walked to the landing at the top of the stairs.

"Mine," she called down. "I slid off the road during the storm the night before last. I haven't had a chance to get a tow out here yet to take care of it. And that little bundle of noise is Simone."

The woman was slim and blonde, dressed in bright red snow pants and a heavy matching parka with navy-blue stripes. She looked at the dog and then looked back at Mimi, her jaw sagging. "You're…"

"A mess," Mimi said quickly. "I know. I was cleaning out one of the rooms upstairs and I'm afraid I tangled with some cobwebs."

She walked down the staircase and held out her hand. "I'm Maura Howard," she said firmly.

The other woman finally closed her mouth, though Mimi could see suspicion still clouding her·blue eyes.

"I'm Easton. Easton Springhill. I've got a ranch down the canyon a ways." Her gaze narrowed and she tilted her head. "This is going to sound crazy, but has anyone ever told you that you look remarkably like that silly woman in the tabloids? Mimi something or other? The one with all the boyfriends?"

Mimi forced a smile she was far from feeling. "I get it all the time. It's a curse, believe me. Ridiculous, isn't she?"

Easton Springhill snickered a little. "I think she's great."

"Really?"

"Sure. She always makes me laugh. No matter what kind of a lousy day I'm having, I can always be glad at least that I'm not as dumb as a box of rocks."

Mimi kept her smile on by sheer force of will. She couldn't really be annoyed. She wasn't stupid, but plenty of her choices certainly had been.

"How did you get here?" she asked instead of snapping at the woman. "Has the snow stopped?"

"It seems to be slowing a little bit. The roads still are a mess but that's not a problem with the snowmobile. I figured I'd better make sure Brant has enough essentials to live on. He doesn't always remember to buy everything he needs for the pantry between visits. I brought over a couple of casseroles from my freezer as well as a few staples I thought he might need. Bread, milk, that sort of thing."

"That's thoughtful of you," Mimi murmured, wondering just what sort of relationship they shared. It must be a close one if the other woman felt comfortable just walking into his house without knocking.

Easton continued gazing at Mimi with that same slightly stunned look in her eyes.

"It's uncanny. The resemblance, I mean."

"Even with the layer of grit I'm wearing from scrubbing the walls upstairs?"

Drawing attention to her less than sleek appearance seemed to convince Easton that she couldn't possibly be Mimi Van Hoyt.

"It's none of my business," the other woman said, "but were you on your way here to see Brant when you crashed? You must have been, I guess. I can't imagine why else you would be on Western Sky land."

"Actually, I thought I was coming to see Gwen Bianca, his caretaker," Mimi answered. "My visit was sort of a whim and I didn't call ahead of time or I would have found out she was out of the country."

"Yes, Gwen has a gallery showing in Milan. She's been working on it for months and was so excited about it."

Her former stepmother had probably told her in one of their occasional phone conversations and Mimi hadn't registered it, maybe because she was a self-absorbed bitch.

She sighed. Past tense. She was turning over a new leaf, right?

"I'm sure Gwen will be so sorry she missed you," Easton said.

"Not as sorry as I am to have missed her, believe me."

"So Brant gave you a place to stay while you wait for her to come back. Isn't that just like him?" She smiled but after a moment it slid away. "Sorry, I'm a little slow today. Back up a minute. If you're a guest of Brant's, why, again, are you covered in grime from scrubbing the walls?"

"I wanted to thank him for his kindness in giving me a place to stay for a few days so I offered to help him out a little."

Easton snickered. "And I actually thought for a minute you were Mimi Van Hoyt. How funny is that?"

Mimi did her best to force a smile. "Hilarious. Not exactly the housecleaning sort, is she?"

Before Easton could answer, the door opened behind them and Brant came into the entry. The open delight on his features when he saw the other woman erased any question that theirs was a close relationship.

"Hey, East!" he said with as close to a genuine smile as Mimi had seen. "I thought I heard a snowmobile."

"Can't sneak up on an Army Ranger, can I?"

"Not on a 600-horsepower Polaris, anyway."

This time he gave a full-fledged grin and Mimi stared. She had thought him handsome before in a clean-cut, no-nonsense sort of way. But when he smiled, he was the kind of gorgeous that curled a woman's toes.

"Any word from the newlyweds?" he asked.

"Tess called me this morning from Costa Rica to thank me again for hosting the wedding on such short notice. She bubbled, you know? I haven't seen her like that since high school."

"I still can't quite believe it." Brant shook his head. "Quinn and the homecoming queen. It boggles my mind."

"I think she's perfect for him."

Since Mimi had no idea whom they were talking about, she thought about edging back up the stairs and returning to her work and leaving them alone, but

Easton seemed to have suddenly remembered she was there.

"Sorry, Maura," the other woman said with a rueful smile. "It's rude of us to talk about people you don't know. A good friend was married two days ago. He was able to coordinate the wedding with Brant's leave so Major Western here could stand up with him."

He was home on leave for a very limited time. Mimi suddenly realized the implications of that fact and she felt every bit the ditzy bimbo everybody believed her to be.

Dumber than a box of rocks, isn't that what Easton said?

She must be or she would have realized that perhaps Brant might have had other plans for his limited leave from a war zone. Instead of enjoying rest and relaxation—and possibly more than that with the very lovely woman who had braved a blizzard for him—he was forced to play host to a stranger. Mimi. A self-absorbed liar who was using him to avoid the unpleasant consequences of her own actions.

She felt small and ashamed and would have been tempted to leave right at that moment if her rental vehicle wasn't still stuck in a creek.

She could at least give them a little privacy now, she thought, even though the idea of the yummy Major Western with this woman made her insides twist unpleasantly.

Just a hint of that blasted morning sickness, she told herself.

"I, um, think I'll just go finish up the bedroom upstairs."

Easton held out an arm. "Wait a minute, Maura. Brant, what are you thinking to make a guest scrub your walls? Gwen or I can hire somebody to do that for you, just like we've always done."

"He's not making me," Mimi protested, disliking the note of censure in the other woman's voice. "I offered to help him prepare the house to sell."

Her words distracted Easton but she didn't look any happier about them than she did the idea of Brant's guest helping him with the cleaning.

"You're really serious about selling, then?"

He looked as if he'd rather be somewhere else. "You know it's for the best, East. The place is falling apart. I can't maintain it when I only come once a year. And as much as I appreciate you and Gwen working so hard to help me, she's moving now and you don't need one more burden now that you're on your own at Winder Ranch."

Easton's mouth clamped into a tight line, as if she were ready to cry. "I hate that everything's changing. If you sell the Western Sky, you won't have any reason to come back."

Feeling excessively like a third wheel, Mimi gave a longing look up the stairs. If she could figure out a way to gracefully escape the two of them without leaving more awkwardness behind, she would.

To her discomfort, Brant folded the woman into his arms, parka and all, and kissed her nose in a tender gesture that had those insides churning again.

"Now you're just being silly," he answered. "You're here. You know I'll always come back for that."

Despite his words, Easton didn't look appeased but she also didn't look as if she wanted to press the issue right now, with "Maura" looking on. "I'd better take off while I still have some daylight. You're going to want to put the food in the fridge."

He tugged the front of her beanie. "Be safe."

"That's my line, Major," she said with a sad sort of smile. "I'll see you again before you ship out."

"Deal."

Her smile widened when she turned to Mimi. "You shouldn't have to work for your room and board. I've got plenty of extra space at my place if you want to bunk there for a few days until Gwen gets back. I'm rattling around out there by myself and wouldn't mind the company at all."

The solution was a logical one, though Mimi was reluctant to take it for reasons she wasn't sure she wanted to examine too closely. "That's very generous of you. But I don't mind the work, really."

Easton looked doubtful. She gave her another long, searching look and she could almost see the other woman thinking how much she looked like, well, herself.

She really hoped Easton didn't say anything to Brant, who just might figure out his houseguest was someone other than she'd claimed.

To her relief, Easton only smiled. "Let me know if you change your mind. It's only a fifteen-minute ride on the Polaris."

"Thank you."

"Call me when you get home so I know you're safe," Brant ordered.

Easton rolled her eyes at him. "I manage by myself three hundred and sixty-five days out of the year, Brant."

"But when I'm here I reserve the right to worry."

"I suppose that's fair since I worry about you every minute of those other three hundred and sixty-five days when you're not."

There was more than just affection between them, Mimi thought as the other woman left. This was a deep, emotional bond.

The realization left her depressed, for reasons she didn't understand.

Chapter Four

Easton left in a swirl of snow and wind and the roar of her powerful snow machine. As Brant closed the door behind her, he couldn't help thinking about the girl she had been, blond braids and freckles and an eager smile as she followed him and Quinn and Cisco around the ranch.

Their foster mother had called them her Four Winds. Like the Four Winds, they had scattered: Quinn Southerland to Seattle, where he ran a shipping company; Cisco Del Norte to Latin America, where he apparently wandered from cantina to cantina doing heaven knows what; and Brant to the Army and five tours of duty in the Middle East in seven years.

Only Easton had stayed. She had been running Winder Ranch for years, even before Jo's death in October.

As much as he still missed Jo, he knew Easton had

it much harder. Her aunt and uncle had raised Easton after her own parents died in a car accident when she was a teenager. Jo had been more than a mother figure to Easton. She had been her best friend and her confidante and he knew Easton had to be terribly lonely without her.

He wished he could make it right but he didn't think the answer was to hang on to his own ranch simply because he knew Easton would be upset when he sold it.

"She's lovely."

He shifted to find Mimi still standing nearby. What surprised him more, he wondered: that he'd forgotten her presence or that she had actually noticed any other woman existed but herself?

Not fair, he admitted with some chagrin. He was judging her purely on her public persona, which so far seemed to be a very different thing than the way she acted away from the cameras.

"She is. Lovely, I mean. And, as usual, she's right to go after me like she did. You shouldn't have to clean for your supper. You're a guest here and I'm not a very good host for allowing you to scrub my walls and clean my toilets."

"Oh, give it a rest, Major. We've been through this."

"It still doesn't seem right."

"Are you saying you think I should take your friend up on her generous offer and stay with her?"

He should agree. He knew it was the proper thing to do and he certainly didn't want Mimi underfoot if she didn't have to be, did he?

But when he opened his mouth to agree and offer to drive her to Winder Ranch on the Western Sky snowmobile, the words seemed to clog in his throat. Despite his better judgment, he didn't want her to go yet. He wasn't quite ready just yet to give up the guilty pleasure of having her here, of watching her in living color.

"It's your call. Either way, you really don't have to clean the house. You can just be a guest. East is right, I can hire somebody to do all this."

"You did hire somebody," she said emphatically. "Me. We made a deal and I'm not going to let you back out of it. If you're sure you want to sell the ranch, I want to help you ready it for the appraisal."

He shouldn't be so relieved, he told himself. But he couldn't help a little inward smile as he headed for the kitchen, shrugging out of his ranch coat as he went. "Well, thanks to East, it looks like we won't starve, even if the blizzard keeps up for days."

"That won't happen, will it?" she asked with wide eyes, though he thought she looked almost relieved at the idea.

He had to wonder again what kind of trouble she might be running away from that she thought his run-down old ranch offered a safe haven. He could only hope it wasn't anything illegal. One of their decorated officers harboring a fugitive might not go over well with the Army brass.

"It's possible for a series of storms to follow one right after the other if we get on the right weather track," he answered as he began putting away the food items Easton had brought over. "When I was a kid, we had one winter where we missed twenty-one days of school because of snow. Storms just kept coming and coming. We spent a miserably short summer that year because of all the make-up days."

She looked so astonished that he couldn't resist needling her. "Did it snow much where you grew up, Ms. Howard?"

She looked blank for only a moment, then quickly recovered. "M-Maura," she said. "I told you I moved around a lot when I was a kid. But never anywhere with this kind of snow. It seems…unreal, somehow."

He definitely agreed with that. Since the moment he'd seen that vehicle head for the creek, he'd somehow slipped into The Twilight Zone.

"Well, I guess I'd better do something about dinner. I'll see if I can throw one of these casseroles Easton brought over into the oven."

"I'll go finish up the bedroom I was cleaning."

He nodded and tried not to look too obvious as he watched her move back up the stairs, her powder puff of a dog following closely behind. She had some silky-looking scarf thing over her hair, a sunny yellow T-shirt and a pair of what he was quite certain were designer jeans that hugged her figure.

More than anything, he suddenly wished that she really *was* Maura Howard and not Mimi Van Hoyt. Maura Howard seemed like a nice woman, someone he would enjoy getting to know a little better. Someone who might not mind that he was a rough-edged Army officer with a tumbledown ranch full of bad memories.

Wouldn't it be nice if she could be just a regular woman who worked for an obscure charitable organization and who preferred cuddling in bed during a blizzard to walking the red carpet at a movie premiere?

He was fiercely attracted to Maura Howard or Mimi Van Hoyt or whoever she was. He wanted to tell himself it was just a normal, red-blooded reaction to a beautiful woman, but the more time he spent with her, the more he was beginning to fear it was more than that.

He sighed and headed for the kitchen. It didn't matter how attracted he was to her. Maura Howard might be polite enough to him during this surreal experience they were sharing. But he had a feeling that since he wasn't a movie star or a minor European prince or some jet-setting playboy, Mimi Van Hoyt wouldn't give him the time of day.

They shared a pretty good dinner of some chicken-and-broccoli pasta dish. Or at least he thought it was good. Mimi didn't eat much and she seemed subdued.

"I think I'll go start tackling the second bedroom upstairs," she said.

"Forget it." He spoke in the same implacable tone his men knew better than to question, but Mimi didn't take the hint.

"Why not?"

"Because you've been on your feet cleaning all day and you look exhausted."

She frowned. "Didn't anyone ever tell you it's not polite to tell a woman she looks less than her best?"

"Didn't anyone ever tell *you* it's not wise to argue with a man who knows a dozen ways to kill an enemy combatant with a dinner fork?"

"Why, Major Western, is that a threat or a joke?"

"I'll let you choose."

She smiled, apparently deciding on the latter. "If you're not careful, I might suspect you have a sense of humor."

He shrugged. "I think it's somewhere buried under all that camouflage."

She smiled again and he wanted to soak it in. Given

the fierce attraction that coiled through him like con-
certina wire, spending the evening with her probably
wasn't the greatest of ideas. He had found every excuse
he could think of all day to avoid spending any great
stretch of time with her, but Brant was suddenly in the
mood to live dangerously.

"Would you like to watch a movie? Or I can go out
and sweep the snow out the satellite dish. There's a
basketball game I wouldn't mind catching tonight."

"Sure. I like basketball," she answered and he suddenly remembered she had once dated one of the Lakers.

When he returned, she was curled up in one corner
of the sofa, looking half-asleep with one of his favorite
thrillers open on her lap. She seemed subdued and he
thought he saw a shadow of sadness in those mossy
green eyes. He wondered again what had brought her
fleeing to Gwen in Idaho without making arrangements
first, then reminded himself it was none of his business.

Though it was always a tricky operation, sweeping
the dish out had done the trick to fix the satellite system
and he quickly tuned in to the game he had hoped to
watch. After a few moments, Mimi set aside her book
and seemed to be engrossed in the game, though he still
thought there was a hint of melancholy in her gaze.

In her understated clothes and with her hair back in
a simple ponytail, she looked a far cry from the sleek
and polished socialite. She looked young and fresh and
so beautiful it was all he could do to stay on his side of
the sofa, to firmly remember they lived in entirely different worlds.

"You know what would make this perfect?" he asked.

She gave him a curious look and he imagined their
definition of perfect probably diverged considerably.

"Popcorn. Buttered popcorn, a fire in the woodstove, a knuckle-biter game on TV and a pretty woman to watch it with me. Do you have any idea how many guys in my entire company would volunteer for latrine duty for a year just for the chance to change places with me right now?"

She smiled a little. "You and your company all apparently have simple tastes, Major."

She was far from simple. He was beginning to think there was far more to Mimi Van Hoyt than a big smile and a lot of flash.

Her silly white dog followed him into the kitchen and lapped at her water and the silver dish of food from the supply Mimi had carried in one of her suitcases.

"Not too much of that water. I don't want Mimi to have to take you out all night," he muttered. The dog yipped at him and wagged her tail and he couldn't help but smile.

The Twilight Zone wasn't necessarily a scary place, just different.

When he returned from the kitchen with two bowls of popcorn, he was relieved to see the score was still tied. He came in just in time to catch a car commercial showing a little nuclear family with a father and mother loading a smiling little toddler into a car seat. Just before they drove away into supposedly happily ever after in their dreamy minivan, the father winked at the toddler, who giggled hard.

Almost instantly, another commercial flashed on, this one for peanut butter, a father and a kid of maybe three sitting together at a kitchen table making sandwiches. The little boy had peanut butter smeared across his mouth and a minute later the camera panned back to the dad, who now had the peanut butter on his cheek where the kid had kissed him.

"Do the advertisers really think all the dads watching the game are going to get right up and make PB and J sandwiches with their kids?" he asked conversationally as he handed her a bowl of popcorn. "With a close game like this, most of them have even forgotten they *have* kids right about now."

To his astonishment, she looked stricken at his words.

"What's the matter?" he asked, trying to figure out what he'd said.

She let out a long breath and manufactured what was obviously a false smile. "Nothing. Nothing at all. Thank you for the popcorn."

She ate very little of it, though, he noticed. And she seemed to have lost most of her interest in the game. After only maybe a quarter of an hour of her picking up a kernel here and there, Simone jumped up and scampered to the door in an obvious signal.

"Don't get up," Mimi said. "I'll put her out."

Simone had made it clear she much preferred going out the back kitchen door. The snow was still deep there but the house's bulk had protected the area from the worst of the snowdrifts.

A few moments later, Mimi returned with the dog in her arms, drying her paws with the towel by the back door he'd reserved for that purpose. "I don't think I can make it to the final buzzer," she said. "I'm just going to maybe take a bath and go to bed."

If he lived to be two hundred, he would never understand women, Brant decided. "How can you leave with a tied score and only two minutes left on the clock?"

She shrugged. "It's been a long day and I was thinking about painting the guest room tomorrow. I found some white paint in the utility room that looks fairly new.

You'd be amazed what a coat of white paint can do for a room with the right accessories. Do you mind?"

"I think you're crazy. You know that, don't you?"

"I think you're absolutely right. I must be or I would have gone back with Easton earlier." She still looked upset, but for the life of him, he couldn't figure out why.

"Why didn't you?"

"Excellent question." She pushed her face into the dog's fur to avoid meeting his gaze. "I like this place, as crazy as that sounds. Simone does, too. There's a sort of peace here. I can't explain it."

He had to think there was some truth to that. By rights, he should hate it here. His childhood had been a difficult time for him, filled with anger and conflict and insecurities. During the bad years, he had dreaded coming home on the school bus. Once he had even stayed on, hunched down on the seat with some vague idea of camping out there until the next morning so he wouldn't have to face his father. His plan might have worked if their old driver, Jesse Richards, hadn't discovered him when he parked the bus for the night at his own place down the canyon.

Despite the bad memories of the Western Sky when he was a kid, he had plenty of good ones, too. When he was out on a mission, this was the place he dreamed about.

So maybe everybody was right. Maybe he should reconsider his decision to sell.

He pushed away the thoughts for now.

"It's just a broken-down ranch house," he answered Mimi. "Yeah, you do sound a little crazy."

"Not the boil-a-rabbit-on-your-stove kind, I promise."

"And wouldn't that be exactly the thing the boil-a-rabbit sort would say?"

She smiled that little smile again, but it didn't quite reach her green eyes. "I'm sure a big, tough Army Ranger like you can take care of himself. But don't worry. I won't even know if you lock your door."

She headed toward her bedroom on the other side of the kitchen and Brant briefly wondered what she would do if he followed her in there and gave in to the low hum of desire he'd been trying to ignore all day.

No, crazy or not, he wouldn't be visiting Mimi Van Hoyt's room anytime soon, he thought, and forced himself to turn back to the game, though it took a superhuman effort.

He might have been able to stick to his pledge to leave her alone if he hadn't heard her crying.

An hour later, Brant stood outside the guest bedroom listening to the quiet weeping coming from the other side of the door. He hissed out a low curse, though he wasn't quite sure if it was aimed more at her or at himself.

He was a sucker for a crying woman. He always had been—maybe because his mother had so seldom cried.

Paula Western had been a master at containing her emotions. Her reaction after Curtis's death had been to turn into herself and shut him and his father out. Except for that single devastating outburst when she had told him she wished he had been the one to drown instead of his baby brother, she had become an empty husk, void of love or affection or emotions of any kind.

He could vividly remember the first time Easton had cried after he moved to Winder Ranch. He had been twelve and Easton was nine, a little tomboy with blond braids living with her parents on the ranch, where her dad was the foreman.

One of the barn kittens had been run over by a tractor driven by a ranch hand. They had all seen it happen but had been too far away to prevent the accident. Easton had been inconsolable and Brant well remembered his panicked compulsion to do something, to fix the situation somehow, even though he knew that particular tragedy had been far beyond anyone's control.

Nothing had changed. He was still compelled to try to fix things, as much as he wanted to hide out and pretend he didn't hear her.

"Mi—Maura?" He caught himself just in time before he would have used her real name. "Everything okay in there?"

The low whimpering stopped. "Yes. Everything's fine."

She didn't say anything else and he sighed, wishing like the devil that he were the sort of guy who could just walk away and leave her to her obvious distress. "Are you sure?"

"Fine."

"Because I could swear I heard someone crying in there."

"I, um, was just humming."

She must think he was the dimmest bulb on the shelf.

"Humming? That's really what you're going with here?"

After another pause, she opened the door a crack and he could see her nose was a little pink, her eyes slightly swollen. He had a feeling Mimi was the sort of woman other females loved to hate for a number of reasons, not least of which was how those subtle signs of distress only made her look impossibly lovely, in a fragile, delicate, take-care-of-me sort of way.

She aimed a glare at him that burst that bubble quickly. "Yes. I was humming. What's it to you?"

He raised his hands in the universal sign of surrender. "You're right. Hum yourself to sleep, for all I care. But here, let me get this teardrop that's not really a teardrop."

He stepped forward and touched his thumb to the skin just at the side of her nose with one finger, where one crystalline bead of moisture pooled.

At his touch, her eyes widened, her gaze caught by his. She was warm and soft, the softest thing he'd ever touched in his life. He wanted nothing more than to slide his hand and cup her chin, to explore the curve of her cheekbone and that delicate shell of an ear.

At that single touch, he wanted to keep touching and touching until he'd explored every inch of delectable skin.

She stared at him for a long, drawn-out moment and he could swear he saw a spark of answering awareness in her eyes. Her dark pupils expanded, until the black nearly overpowered the green. He leaned forward just a hair and she caught her breath.

The instant before his mouth would have found hers, reality exploded like a shoulder-fired missile in his head. Kissing her would only make this hunger in his gut all the more painfully intense, only make him more cognizant of what he was missing.

He dropped his hand and forced himself to throttle back.

He thought he saw disappointment flicker in her eyes, but she stepped away and lowered her eyes. "I'm sorry if I disturbed you. It won't happen again, I promise."

"Does that mean you're done or just that you'll keep your…humming to yourself from now on?"

She didn't answer, just seemed to grip the door that much harder. "Good night, Brant."

He knew it was corny but hearing her say his name in that throaty voice sent heat rippling through his insides.

For a long, protracted moment, he stared at her standing there in a soft, pale green nightgown that only seemed to make her eyes look more vivid. He still wanted to kiss her, with a heat and urgency that shocked him. But he had learned a long time ago that just because he wanted something didn't make it good for him.

Chapter Five

"Are you sure you're going to be okay now? No more…humming?"

Mimi gazed at him, so big and commanding and decent. For one insane moment, she wanted to throw herself against that powerful chest and sob out everything, all the lousy choices she had made that led her to this place up to this moment.

She was appalled at herself for breaking down—and for doing it where she had a potential audience.

It had to be the hormones. She hadn't meant to cry. When Brant had been making popcorn earlier, a promo for one of the entertainment news shows had come on, touting their insider coverage of the fifty-thousand-dollar Vera Wang dress Jessalyn was going to wear in only a few days' time.

She probably would have been just fine with that, but

then in rapid succession during halftime had come two sappy commercials showing sweet-as-cotton-candy interactions of fathers and their children, highlighting even more clearly what she knew her child would have to do without.

Even with that, she might have been able to hold back the crying fest. But after her bath, as she had been pulling a nightgown on she had caught sight of her tiny, barely noticeable baby bump in the mirror and out of nowhere she had been overwhelmed with a combination of fierce joy and abject terror.

She was only hormonal, she reminded herself. That's the reason tears seemed to threaten at the oddest moments these days.

She had never been much of a crier, since she had learned early that her tears had absolutely no effect on Werner Van Hoyt. He would look down his aquiline nose in that slightly bored look he'd perfected, glance at his antique Patek Philippe, and then ask her if she was quite finished yet.

But here was Brant Western, a man she barely knew, showing up at her bedroom door with a slightly panicked but determined look on his face at the sound of her tears. Instead of ignoring her and walking by, as most sane men would probably do when confronted with a strange woman's weeping, he stopped and knocked to ask if she was all right.

Sharing her fears with *someone* would be so comforting, but she couldn't tell him, of course.

She barely knew the man. How could she just blurt out that she'd had an affair with an engaged Grammy winner who was getting married in a few days, that she was now pregnant from said affair, and that she planned to keep the child and raise it on her own, despite the father's strident objections?

Framed so bluntly, it all sounded so stark and sordid. And once she put some of it into words, she was afraid she would blurt out everything. Her identity, Marco's, all the stupid choices that had led her to this moment, and then Major Western would despise her, as well he should.

When he touched her cheek with such tenderness to wipe away the tear she claimed didn't exist, she thought she had seen a spark of male interest in his eyes. But of course she couldn't have. He and the so-beautiful Easton had feelings for each other and Mimi had made a personal vow that she would never allow herself to become involved with another woman's man.

Been there, done that. She'd been the "other woman" only once in her life, with Marco—though she knew rumors said otherwise—and she wasn't about to repeat the experience, no matter how tempting the package.

"I'm fine. Good night, Major."

She closed the door firmly behind her, then leaned against it. As tempting as it was, she couldn't spill everything to Brant. She was on her own now. She couldn't count on anybody but herself.

Not her father, not feckless celebrities who cheated on their betrothed with other feckless celebrities, and certainly not soldiers she barely knew who watched her with quiet blue eyes and offered an entirely too appealing shoulder to cry upon.

The snow was still falling when she awoke the next morning. The light outside her window was murky and pale but she could see through a gap in the curtains that soft flakes continued to drift down.

Maybe the snow would continue to fall and fall and fall and she would never have to return to real life.

She couldn't hide out here forever. Eventually she would have to face the consequences of her decision. Her father would have to know. He would no doubt be gravely disappointed in her. Nothing new there.

She didn't care. She would weather that storm like this old ranch weathered all the Idaho winters.

She touched her abdomen. "We'll tough it out together, kiddo," she said out loud, waking up Simone.

The dog stretched and yawned, then jumped off the bed to the floor and skittered to the door, where she stood wagging her tail insistently in a clear indication of her needs.

Mimi sighed and reached for her robe. She cautiously opened her bedroom door and peered out into the hall. She did *not* want to encounter her host yet this morning, not when she was still so mortified about her emotional breakdown the night before.

To her relief, Brant wasn't anywhere in sight, so she quickly let Simone outside. When she opened the door, she saw that the snow had indeed slowed but the drifts had to be higher than her waist in places.

It would take them days to dig out, she thought happily. Real life could wait at least a few days longer.

She showered quickly after letting Simone back inside and spent only twenty minutes on her hair and makeup, definitely some kind of record. Her stylist Giselle would probably blow a gasket if she caught Mimi with her hair a frizzy mess and wearing only barebones foundation and mascara.

She didn't care. She gazed into the round warped mirror in the bathroom. What did she need with Giselle?

She thought she looked good. She had gained a little weight with the baby but for the first time since she hit adolescence, she thought a little extra weight wasn't necessarily a bad thing on her. It filled in some of the hollows of her features, made her almost lush.

Brant still hadn't returned to the house by the time Mimi finished a quick breakfast, so she headed up to the larger upstairs bedroom.

Now that the snow had begun to clear just a little, she had a fantastic view from up here of the west slope of the Tetons, jagged and raw in the distance. It was a breathtaking vista and she thought that if she owned the ranch, she would make this her bedroom and position her bed looking out so that she could always wake to that view.

She caught her breath at the idea. What if *she* bought the Western Sky? It would be a wonderful place to raise a baby, surrounded by dogs and horses and those mountains.

Once planted, the idea refused to die and as she prepped the room for paint, she had great fun imagining what changes she might make if she had full reign here.

A new kitchen would be at the top of her list. And perhaps she would take that wide porch off the back and screen it in so that she could sit out there on summer evenings while the baby played on the floor.

"You weren't lying about the humming."

Mimi gasped and whirled around to find Brant in the doorway looking tall and gorgeous and completely yummy. How had she missed hearing him come in?

She aimed a glare at Simone for not warning her but the little dog only bared her teeth in her version of an embarrassed smile for slacking on her guard-dog duties.

"I never lie," she lied.

A tiny dimple appeared in the corner of his mouth. "Is that right?"

Just about every word she had said to him since she arrived had either been a half-truth or an outright fib—or had concealed something she hadn't wanted him to know—but she decided to keep that information to herself.

"You must have left the house early. Is everything okay?"

"I was just checking the pipes at Gwen's. So far no breaks in the line. I heard from the furnace company and they're going to try to schedule the job Friday."

"That's good."

"Did you have breakfast?"

"I grabbed a cup of tea and some toast."

"I made fresh coffee."

"I saw it." And she had craved some desperately but she had read in one of those secret pregnancy books that she should avoid caffeine during the pregnancy. She had also read to avoid oil-based paints. To her relief, the cans she found were all water-based.

Funny how there was nothing in the books about avoiding gorgeous soldiers with wide shoulders and elusive smiles. He looked tired, she thought. But then, his eyes had looked tired since she arrived.

"I saw the snow seems to have eased a little bit," she said.

"Some. According to the forecast, it should snow until mid-morning and then we can start the fun of digging out."

"That's a relief, I'm sure."

"I don't know if I'd say that but at least we'll be able to get your car fixed."

She wasn't convinced that was something to stick in

the positive column. "When do you have to report back to the Army?"

"Tuesday."

"Less than a week. Oh, Brant, I'm so sorry. You've had to spend your entire free time playing host to a guest you hadn't expected and don't want. It was supremely selfish of me to intrude like this, to just assume I wouldn't be in the way. You have only a few days to call your own and I ruined everything for you."

To her deep mortification, her throat swelled with tears and she again cursed the pregnancy hormones.

He tilted his head, studying her with a puzzled sort of concern. "Please don't start humming again."

She managed a watery laugh and focused on thinking about baby names until she was calmer. "I'm sorry. I'll spare you that, at least."

He was silent for a moment to give her a chance to compose herself, a small courtesy she found touching and thoughtful.

"You've already been busy this morning," he said.

"I think I'm just about ready to start painting."

"Do you need some help?"

She should just tell him now and push him out the door. But it was his house, after all. If he wanted to spend his limited leave with a paintbrush in his hand, how could she possibly stop him?

"You've lucked out. I've already done the hardest part, the prep work. I'm just about ready to start painting." She held up the angled brush she'd found with the paint supplies in the storage room. "Do you want to roll or cut in the edges?"

"I'm assuming that by the sound of it, cutting in the edges takes some skill with a paintbrush, which is something I'm sorry to say I don't possess. I think I should be able to handle a roller without any major catastrophes."

She smiled and handed him the paint roller she had also found in the utility room. "Just remember that you offered."

He seemed to be wading deeper and deeper into The Twilight Zone.

An hour later, Brant finished rolling paint on the last section of wall and stood back to survey the work.

Mimi stood on a ladder, her arms above her head as she angled the brush carefully to keep the paint away from the ceiling and trim.

Who would have guessed that Mimi Van Hoyt even knew how to hold a paintbrush, forget about how to wield it so expertly. When in her pampered life would she possibly have had the opportunity to paint a room? He would have thought her father hired teams of high-priced designers for projects like this.

The woman was a complete mystery to him. He wanted to ask what she was *really* doing in Cold Creek Canyon. Who or what was she running from? What was behind that little glimmer of sadness he sometimes caught in her eyes, those tears she hadn't been at all successful in hiding the night before?

At this point, he was going to have to come right out and ask her since all his subtle attempts to extract information had led him to dead end after dead end.

No matter what he asked or how he asked it, she somehow deflected every question, until he had no clearer idea what she might be doing there than he had when she showed up.

He had questioned hardened enemy combatants who weren't as adept at avoiding the truth as Mimi Van Hoyt.

He found her fascinating. Everything about her, from the way she nibbled on her bottom lip while she concentrated on a tricky corner to the way she focused completely on his face when he was talking to the lush curves that gave him entirely inappropriate ideas when she was climbing up and down the ladder.

Nobody would ever believe she was actually here in his ramshackle house, with her curly dark hair tied back in a ponytail and a tiny spray of paint splattering her cheek like white freckles.

He couldn't quite believe it—nor was he particularly thrilled about the way he couldn't seem to stop watching her.

At least for the last hour, she had completely distracted him from the pain and guilt that seemed to follow him everywhere.

"You were right," he said a moment later as he slid the roller back into the tray.

"I was? About what?" She sounded as surprised as if she'd spent her entire existence being told otherwise.

"About the paint. I'm amazed at what a difference a simple whitewash can make. It looks like a whole new room."

"Wait until we put the second coat up. I was thinking I'll move the furniture around a little bit to take advantage of that stellar view. If you angle the bed a little, the first thing your guests will see are those mountains out there. And what do you think about moving that watercolor that's in the hallway where it's too dark to be appreciated? It would fit right there on the south wall."

He gave her a careful look. "You're into this, aren't you?"

She blinked at him from her perch atop the ladder. "What?"

"Giving new life to this old place."

She looked taken aback at first, and then slowly considering as she climbed down the ladder. "I do enjoy it," she said, wiping her hands on a rag. "I told you I've done it before. A friend of mine from school flips houses in L.A. and she sometimes lets me help her stage the place for an open house."

"In between your charity work." He must have missed the paparazzi coverage of her renovating an old house.

"This is just a hobby. You know. For fun."

Before he had become acquainted with her these past few days, he would have thought her whole life was about having fun. After spending a little time in her company, he wasn't so sure. He had a feeling life hadn't been the smooth sail for Mimi that people seemed to think.

"Marisa calls me whenever she needs another set of hands. It gets me out of my routine, you know? A change of pace."

"Have you thought about doing this as a career? Staging houses, I mean?"

"I couldn't!" she exclaimed. "I don't know the first thing about what I'm doing."

"That hasn't stopped you here."

She gazed at him, her eyes a deep, startled green. "You really think I could?"

"Why not?"

"Why not." She looked rather dazed by the idea and he wondered just what he might have unleashed.

"I never thought… I mean, I'm always glad to help Marisa. We always have a good time, but that's just her telling me what to do."

"You don't have anybody telling you what to do here. How to place the furniture or hang the pictures or whatever."

"You're right." She smiled then, that radiant smile he couldn't get enough of, the one the public seemed to adore. "That is a really interesting idea, Major. I'm going to have to give it some thought."

He managed a smile in return, even though his insides were jumping around like sand fleas.

"You've got a little bit of paint on your nose."

"Where?"

"Not so much a smudge as a few tiny splatters. You look like you've got white freckles."

Color rose along her cheekbones, making the spots stand out in stark relief, much to his astonishment. She took the cloth, found a clean corner, and started dabbing at her face, but in completely the wrong spot.

If the idea of her exploring the possibility of going into the real estate business was a good one, this ranked right up there on the opposite side of the spectrum. It was a phenomenally dangerous impulse but Brant couldn't seem to stop himself from stepping forward and taking the cloth from her hands.

"No. Here. Let me."

He dabbed along the side of her nose and then just along the angled ridge of her cheekbone.

His fingers brushed her skin as they had the night before and he heard her sharp intake of breath, but he was too busy fighting back his own fierce hunger to cup her face in his hands and press his mouth fiercely to hers.

A smart man would turn around and walk out of the room. No, a smart man would just keep on going until he'd put another zip code between himself and a dangerous woman like Mimi Van Hoyt.

But right now he didn't feel very smart. He suddenly ached to taste her, just once. She was a soft, beautiful woman and he was a hardened soldier who had been far too long without much sweetness in his life.

Years from now, when he saw her in the newsstands, looking polished and beautiful and worlds away from his life, he could remember how their worlds had once intersected just for a moment.

He stepped forward and lowered his head. One kiss, he told himself. What could possibly be the harm?

She tasted sweet and sensual at the same time, like deep, rich chocolate drizzled over vanilla ice cream.

For a good ten seconds, she stood frozen like a spear of ice as his mouth moved over hers. At first, she didn't exactly respond but she didn't jerk away in outrage, either. As he deepened the kiss, she seemed to give a little shiver, her hands gripping his shirt, and he felt the seductive slide of her tongue against his. And then she was kissing him with as much wild heat as he could have ever dreamed.

He was hard in an instant. How could he not be? She was soft and warm and the most beautiful woman he'd ever seen in his life and she was right here in his arms, kissing him like she never wanted him to stop.

Chapter Six

She was sinking, sinking, sinking.

For long, wondrous moments, Mimi let herself be carried away on the slow, leisurely current of this delicious attraction. His mouth was firm and determined on hers and he was big and solid and muscled and she just wanted to nestle against him and stay here forever.

Gradually, a tiny hint of reason began to flutter cautiously through her, like a tiny moth unfurling its wings for the first time.

She wanted so much to ignore it, to swat at the annoying little thing until it disappeared. In his arms she could be Maura Howard, someone good and decent. Someone much better than she was.

She wanted to stay right here in his arms. For now, the only important thing was the two of them and this delicious heat between them, sliding around and through her like a ribbon of river cutting through a steep canyon.

Brant kissed like a man who put a great deal of thought and energy into it. He seemed to know just how to dance his mouth across hers, just where to slide that tongue.

She wrapped her arms around his back, soaking in the solid strength of his muscles and the scent of him, of laundry soap and some sort of sage and cedar aftershave and the underlying sharpness of paint around them.

More than anything, she wanted to stay in this room kissing him while the snow drifted down in lazy flakes outside. But that annoying moth of a conscience continued to flutter at the edge of her thoughts until she couldn't ignore it any longer.

Easton. Brant had feelings for his beautiful neighbor, with the sleek blond hair and the big blue eyes.

He belonged to someone else and Mimi had no right to kiss him like this. She couldn't do this again. She *wouldn't*. She had just spent three terrible, guilt-ridden months in a furtive relationship with a man who was committed to someone else.

She had believed Marco when he told her his engagement with Jessalyn was just for show, that he didn't love her, that he would figure out a way to break things off before the wedding.

She had known, somewhere deep inside, that he was lying to her, but she had been too caught up in the thrill of the moment and had ignored the voice of reason.

She couldn't ignore it now.

She was going to be someone's mother in six months. Wasn't it past time that she became someone she could like and respect? Tangling tongues with a man whose heart belonged to someone else didn't seem the way to achieve that particular goal.

She closed her eyes, fighting the part of her that just wanted to hang on tight to Brant, to absorb a little of his strength.

No. She needed to stand on her own, to find her own strength.

"Stop."

To her grave chagrin, instead of sounding tough and determined, the word came out a tiny squeak, one she wasn't sure he even heard.

She drew in a breath and tried again.

"Stop!" The second time, the word came out overloud, especially in the quiet bedroom, and Brant froze.

After a long moment, he groaned and wrenched his mouth away and for a long moment they stood bare inches apart, their breathing heavy and their gazes locked.

The raw hunger in his eyes sent an answering throb humming through her. She was so very tempted to smash that little moth of conscience under her shoes and just plunge back into the heat of his arms. But if she couldn't find the strength to do the right thing now, however was she going to stand up against her father and all the others who would have a problem with her pregnancy?

"I don't want this." Her voice wobbled a little but it still held a note of determination. "Not with you."

She saw disbelief and even a little hurt in his eyes before he shuttered his expression. After another moment, he stepped away. "Apparently I misread some kind of sign."

She closed her eyes so she didn't reveal to him that

he had misread *nothing*. She had wanted him to kiss her, had craved it desperately.

If she hadn't listened to that blasted fledgling conscience, she would still be wrapped around him. The shame of just how much she still wanted to ignore it turned her voice sharper than she had intended.

"Why would you just jump to the conclusion that I'm the sort of woman who would start tangling tongues with someone she barely knows?"

He gave her a long look. "I don't know. Maybe because that's just what you *did?*"

Her mouth tightened and she opted to go on the offensive. "You took me by surprise and didn't give me a chance to react. I was too stunned to push you away."

"So your hands in my hair and your tongue in my mouth, that was just you being stunned?"

She glared. "I did not come to Idaho to start something with some soldier just trying to hit on anybody warm and willing while he's home on leave."

She immediately regretted the words, especially when his color rose and his jaw tightened. He suddenly looked rough and hardened, every inch a warrior. Not a wise move, taunting a man who lived a dangerous life she couldn't even imagine, especially when she was alone here at his ranch and completely at his mercy.

Easton was the only person who knew for certain where she was, she suddenly realized.

He wouldn't hurt her, she told herself, though the hard anger in his eyes wasn't an encouraging sign.

"Well, you're obviously not willing," he said in a lethally soft voice. "And not particularly warm, either, when it comes to that. My mistake."

She had wounded him, she realized, by implying

any woman would do as well as the next one. For a moment, she wanted to apologize, but then she remembered Easton and the obvious affection between the two of them and she glared right back at him.

"Now that we know where we stand, I'm going to go out and check on the horses and see if I can start clearing away some of the snow yet."

The sooner you leave, the better. He didn't say the words but she caught the subtext anyway.

After he stalked out of the room, she eased onto the edge of the bed, to the slick plastic she had found to protect the furnishings in the room from the paint.

She had never been kissed like that, with such fierce concentration, such raw intensity. She touched a finger to her lips and closed her eyes, reliving the heat and wonder of it.

After a long moment, she opened her eyes and slid from the bed with a crackle of plastic. Enough. She had to get back to work and forget the past few moments ever happened, though she had a feeling that was going to be a harder task than scrubbing every inch of his old house.

Brant didn't come inside at all for lunch, something that left her feeling both grateful and guilty—grateful for the space and distance between them right now but guilty over the idea of him going hungry. She could hear the rumble of some sort of heavy machinery outside, and once she had peeked out the window and saw him on a powerful-looking tractor pushing snow with smooth, practiced motions.

Simone jumped up on a chair near the window in the kitchen and watched Brant on the tractor as if she'd never seen anything quite so fascinating.

Mimi knew just how her dog felt. She sighed and dumped the rest of her sandwich into the garbage.

The second coat in the bedroom took her less than an hour since she didn't need to be as precise around the edges. He still hadn't returned to the house by the time she finished cleaning up the brushes and the roller and returning the paint supplies to the utility room. After she finished, she realized she was exhausted, another of those little pregnancy joys.

A small nap was definitely in order, she decided, before she tackled the upstairs bathroom.

When she awoke, she was astonished to see she had slept for two hours and the light outside her bedroom was pale with late-afternoon sun.

Some days back in L.A., she wouldn't even get up until two or three in the afternoon so she could go clubbing all night. She couldn't go back to that world, ever. She didn't want to, even if everything hadn't changed with that simple pregnancy test.

That world, the endless quest for fun and excitement, had all seemed so vital. Now she could clearly see how very empty her life had been.

She was twenty-six years old and didn't know the first thing about responsibility. She had somehow squeaked her way to a degree in public relations and marketing from UCLA, probably because her father had donated a large sum to the university, but she had no idea what to do with her education.

She thought of Brant's suggestion that she consider staging houses. Real estate. Mimi shook her head. Maybe she had inherited more from her father than green eyes and a temper. Still, it was exciting to think about the possibilities.

Her stomach rumbled a bit and she realized the two bites of sandwich she'd eaten at lunch just weren't enough now that she was eating for two and had to consider things like folic acid and calcium intake.

She took a little extra care in the bathroom with her hair and makeup then stood at the mirror for a long moment, wary of walking out into the kitchen and facing Brant again.

Their easy companionship of the morning while they had worked together painting seemed a long time ago and she wasn't looking forward to the tension she feared would tug between them now that they'd kissed.

She couldn't hide out here in the bathroom hugging an old-fashioned bowl sink forever, she reminded herself. She could handle whatever challenges life threw at her, even in the form of a mouthwatering man who gave her entirely inappropriate ideas.

She opened the door to her bedroom and heard him in the kitchen before she saw him. He was talking on the phone and though she didn't intend to eavesdrop, she couldn't help but hear his words.

"I know I told you I would try to make it down for a few days, Abby, but this has been a bear of a storm and there have been…complications at the ranch."

Abby? Yet another woman? She frowned. The man did get around. But then, he'd been in the Middle East for several months and she imagined dating opportunities weren't exactly thick on the ground there.

Mimi frowned as she suddenly realized *she* was the complication he was talking about at the ranch that made it difficult for him to leave to visit his apparently endless string of honeys.

"Yeah, I understand," Brant was saying. "I'm sorry

things haven't worked out like I planned. But I'm still flying out of Salt Lake City and my flight doesn't leave until late Tuesday. What if I come down in the morning and spend the day before I have to be at the airport? A short visit is better than nothing."

He was quiet as Abby, whoever she was, must have responded. "Yeah," he said after a moment. "I know, sweetheart. It's not fair. I hate it, too."

His voice sounded not regretful in the way of a man breaking a date but tight, almost bleak.

"Yeah, I'll call you. Hugs to the girls from me. Love you."

After a long moment of silence from the kitchen, Mimi tried to walk nonchalantly into the room. She didn't know what she expected to see but it wasn't the strong and capable Brant Western sitting at the kitchen table with her dog in his lap, his features tight with pain and a sorrow she couldn't begin to guess at.

She froze in the doorway, not quite sure how to react to the sight of his obvious turmoil. She would have slipped back down the hall to her bedroom before he caught sight of her but Simone barked and scampered off his lap, bounding into her arms.

By the time she had picked up her dog and given the requisite love, as inconvenient as the distraction was, Brant had schooled his features.

He could tell she had heard, she realized, as he moved away from the table and dumped the dregs of his coffee mug into the sink. She didn't think it was an accident that he avoided her gaze.

He obviously wanted to pretend nothing was wrong but she had never been very good at keeping her mouth shut, even when she knew darn well it was a mistake to speak.

"Having girlfriend trouble?"

He looked baffled. "Girlfriend?"

"On the phone. I heard the tail end of your conversation."

His eyes widened and he stared at his phone and then back at Mimi. "Abby? No! She's not... We're not..."

He looked aghast at the very idea and Mimi shrugged, knowing she shouldn't be so relieved. One girlfriend was enough. "None of my business. You just seemed upset. That was the logical conclusion."

"Well, you were wrong."

"Oh?"

He narrowed his gaze at her and she saw anger there and something deeper, something dark and almost anguished. "Abby is smart and warm and lovely, but she isn't my girlfriend. She's the widow of one of my men."

"Oh." Her small exclamation sounded unusually loud in the sudden hush of the kitchen. "My mistake."

"Right." He paused. "Ty Rigby was a damn good soldier. He was killed three weeks ago in an ambush, along with two other of my most trusted men."

She stood frozen as the words poured out of him like thick, ugly sludge. "As we were fighting to keep him from bleeding to death, he asked me to watch out for his wife and his two little girls. I'm doing a hell of a job, aren't I?"

"Oh, Brant. I'm so sorry." The words seemed painfully inadequate as she saw the torment in his eyes, the weight of responsibility in him.

She thought of her life, the shopping and the gossip and the parties. While he was risking his life and watching his friends die, she was complaining about eye shadow and the new girl who did her pedicures all wrong and how some restaurant had taken her favorite thing off the menu.

"Bad enough that Abby has lost her husband, but now she's facing financial problems. She's probably going to lose the house. She doesn't have a college degree and even with Ty's death benefits, it's going to be a real struggle for her to make it the next few years while the kids are little."

Mimi sank into a chair, her mind racing as she tried to figure out how she could fix things for the poor woman without revealing that she had more money than she could ever spend in a hundred lifetimes.

"Why doesn't she come here?" she suddenly suggested. "You've got a house that sits empty all the time. She could bring her kids and take care of the house in exchange for rent. It's the perfect solution!"

He looked astonished and rather impressed. "I actually had the same idea," he admitted. "I offered it to her but Abby's a proud woman and she refused. Besides that, her family and Ty's are in Utah and she doesn't want to leave that support cushion right now. She'll probably go live with her parents until she can get back on her feet. She won't be homeless. But she won't have her husband, either."

His voice was grim, desolate, and Mimi chewed her lip, disgusted with herself for the angry thoughts she'd had about him earlier.

"That's the reason I was thinking about selling the ranch. I thought maybe I could, I don't know, maybe set up a trust or something to help. I guess you'd know more about that, since you work for a charitable foundation, right?"

She opened her mouth to respond, wondering why

he used such a harsh, goading tone, but he didn't give her a chance.

"It's a crazy idea," he went on. "But I feel really helpless about the whole thing."

"And responsible?" she guessed.

He scraped his chair back from the table and stood quickly. "I need to head back out and see if I can at least finish clearing out the driveway. I don't know if I'll be back inside before it gets dark out there so go ahead and find what you want for dinner. I just ate a late lunch so I won't be hungry for a while."

"Okay." She forced a smile but he was already heading to the mudroom and didn't turn back around.

What had she said that hit such a hot button? she wondered as he stalked from the kitchen.

Why couldn't he have just kept his big mouth shut?

Brant stomped outside into the bitterly cold afternoon, shoving on his work gloves as he went.

Mimi didn't give a rat's rear end about a bunch of soldiers in a world thousands of miles away from her pampered existence. She had more important things to think about, like her next movie premiere.

A woman like her couldn't possibly understand the gritty, hazardous irrevocability of his world. So why had he told her? The words had just bubbled out and he hadn't been able to stop them.

She hadn't reacted quite as he might have guessed. He had seen shock in her eyes, certainly, but also an unexpected empathy. For a moment, he had wanted to spew all of it to her. His pain and his guilt and the grief for his friends.

Somehow it was only too easy to forget who she was

when they were alone here at the ranch. He almost couldn't believe the woman who teased him and scrubbed his walls and spent the morning painting his spare bedroom was the same flighty, shallow publicity-hungry ditz the tabloids seemed so enamored with.

She had kissed him with passion and an urgent heat and then she had pushed him away, accusing him of being some sex-starved bastard putting the moves on any woman who breathed at him.

That had stung, he admitted. And absolutely wasn't true. He had kissed her because he hadn't been able to think about anything else all morning long as they worked together painting the room.

He didn't know what to think of her. Which was the mask and which was the real woman?

None of his business, he reminded himself as he started the tractor, which sputtered to life with a low rumble. In a few days, he would be returning to duty and she would be Gwen Bianca's problem. He would never see her again and this strange interlude would simply be a story for him to tell his men on boring transports.

That was what he wanted, right? So why did the thought of never seeing her again leave him feeling as cold and empty as the February sky?

Chapter Seven

The room looked fantastic, if she did say so herself.

An hour after Brant left in such a hurry to return to the endless task of shoveling snow, Mimi stood on the second to top rung of the stepladder in the newly painted bedroom, trying to rehang the curtains.

Lucky for her the paint had been fast-drying so she could start the fun process of returning the furnishings and really making a difference in the room.

The new coat of paint had brightened the room considerably, making everything look fresh and cheerful. She had found a lovely deep blue crazy quilt in the linen closet and decided to use that as the focal point of the room.

On the top shelf of the bedroom closet, she had unearthed a goldmine of dusty antique bottles of various sizes and shapes in deep jewel tones, including several in a blue that nearly identically matched the quilt. She washed them out with dish soap and water and set them along the frame of the double-paned windows, where they glowed as they caught the pale afternoon light.

She had hung the same now-clean curtains but decided they needed something extra. A further search of the attic found a length of fabric in a pale blue, long enough to use as a graceful swag above the other drapes.

It would be a small change, maybe, but sometimes tiny changes had the power to rock the world. Just look at her pregnancy.

Okay, it had rocked *her* world. But wasn't that enough for now?

She reached to arrange a fold that wasn't quite even and she wasn't exactly sure what happened next. She must have leaned just a few inches too far, upsetting her balance, or perhaps the ladder tilted on an uneven spot on the carpet at just the moment she was off-kilter.

Whatever happened, one moment she was reaching across the window to adjust the curtain, the next she was tumbling down, taking the fabric and a few of the antique bottles with her.

She hit the ground, her gasp frozen in her throat as her lungs froze at the impact.

Even as she panicked and fought to catch her breath, pain screamed out from her right side and she realized she must have banged against the small square table she had situated beneath the window to be used as a writing desk.

Simone barked and rushed toward her, her little body wriggling and her black eyes wide with concern. She licked at Mimi's face and the action of that tiny wet tongue on her skin seemed to jolt her lungs back to action, for some strange reason.

She lay on the floor, focusing only on inhaling and

exhaling for several long moments before she dared move to scoop the anxious dog against her.

She hurt everywhere.

Her head, her side, the wrist that she had instinctively thrown out to catch her fall.

Several shards of broken glass from the bottles were embedded in her palm and blood dropped onto the carpet until she pulled it across her chest so it could drip on her shirt.

At the movement, a heavy cramp suddenly spasmed across her lower stomach and then another, so intense, she had to curl up. For several endless moments, she couldn't think past the sudden raw, consuming panic.

No. Oh, please. Dear God, no.

"You're okay, kiddo," she whispered, her words a ragged whimper. "You're all right. I'm sorry. I'm so sorry. It was an accident."

Her abdomen cramped again, a rippling wave that took what was left of her breath.

Simone whined, snuggling closer, and Mimi clung to her.

She couldn't lose this baby. Not after she had reached the monumental decision that she wanted it so very desperately. She needed help. A doctor. She had to find Brant. He would help her. Oh, why hadn't she asked for his cell phone number?

Through her panic, she heard a steady rumble outside. The tractor. He must be plowing closer to the house.

Though the very magnitude of the task overwhelmed her, she knew she had to somehow make her way down the stairs and out into the bitter cold to attract Brant's attention so he could help her.

The next few moments were a blur of pain and fear

as she made her way slowly through the house, one painful step at a time.

By the time she reached the front door, she was breathing hard and soaked with sweat from the effort. Her abdomen had cramped twice more and she'd had to stop each time as the pain washed over and through her.

Finally she reached the front door. When she staggered to it and yanked it open, Simone raced out and off the porch, barking furiously on the shoveled sidewalk.

The dog's urgent call for attention might have been more effective if she wasn't a tiny white dog standing amid all that snow, but Mimi still appreciated the effort. She moved to the edge of the porch and grabbed the nearest column as the cold sucked at her bones.

The tractor had an enclosed cab and she knew he wouldn't hear her yelling over the machine's noise, so she waved her uninjured arm as much as she could, blood dripping from her other hand to fall in stark contrast to the snow.

After what felt like the longest moments of her life, her efforts finally paid off. Brant caught sight of her and shut off the tractor. Mimi didn't think she had ever heard a sweeter sound than the sudden silence, and she knew she had never felt such relief when Brant leaped from the tractor and raced toward her, faster than she would have believed possible.

"You're bleeding. What happened?"

"I fell…off the ladder." She could barely squeeze the words out through her fear. "The baby. Oh, please, I… need a doctor."

He stared at her. "Baby? Baby! You're pregnant?"

She gave a tiny nod, all she could manage, and an instant later he scooped her into his arms and carried her back into the house.

"I'm cramping. It started right after I fell. Oh, please. I don't want to lose my baby. Please help me, Brant."

His face looked carved in granite as he carried her to the family room and laid her gently on the sofa. The fire's warmth soaked into her, warming her from the chill of the outside air, but it did nothing for the iciness in her heart.

"Let me call Jake Dalton and see what we should do."

We. Why had she never realized what vast comfort could be contained in the simple word?

He covered her with the throw from the back of the couch and Simone snuggled against her. Mimi closed her eyes, grateful beyond words that he was a strong, determined, take-charge man, since she barely had a coherent thought in her head beyond her terror.

"Maggie," Brant said urgently into the phone, "this is Brant Western. Yes. I was calling for Jake but you can help me out here. I've got someone staying at my ranch who just fell off a stepladder. She's pregnant and she says she's cramping. What should we do?"

He was quiet for a moment, listening to something on the other end, then he turned to Mimi. "How far along are you?" he asked Mimi. Though she could still see the shock in his eyes, she recognized he was no stranger at adjusting to the unexpected.

"Eleven weeks," she answered. "That's what the doctor said anyway."

He relayed the information to this Maggie person, paused a moment, then turned back to Mimi.

"What about, uh, bleeding?"

If she weren't so terrified she might have smiled at this sign of his discomfort at the intimacy of their discussion. Instead, she only shook her head.

"Negative," he answered into the phone, a look of obvious relief on his features.

"I'll get her there," he said after a moment, his words sounding like a solemn vow. "I can't guarantee how long it will take us to get down the canyon, but we'll make it as soon as we can. Yeah. Okay. Thanks, Mag. See you."

He hung up and turned back to Mimi. "Maggie Dalton is the nurse practitioner at the clinic. Her husband is the town doctor. She thinks it's best to have an ultrasound and check everything out. Are you up for a ride to town?"

"Anything, as long as they can help me. Can we make it through the snow?"

"One of the ranch pickups has a plow. I can't promise you the most comfortable ride you've ever had and it might take us some time, but we'll get there."

"Thank you." Her abdomen cramped again and she folded both arms around it and gave a little moan.

His eyes reflected something close to panic. "Hang on," he said. "You're going to have to give me a couple minutes to get the truck out of the garage and drive it up here. Just wait here and I'll come help you outside."

She nodded and hugged Simone to her, praying fiercely the entire time he was gone. It was probably only five minutes or so but each second seemed endless.

When he returned, he spent another few moments putting a reluctant Simone in her crate and helping Mimi into her coat, and then before she quite realized what he intended, he scooped her into his arms and carried her outside to an aging blue pickup truck with an extended cab.

"I would suggest you lie down on the backseat but, with the snowy conditions, you're going to need to wear your seat belt and you can't do that lying down. I'm sorry."

"It's fine. Just go."

As soon as she was settled, he backed the truck up and headed down the driveway at a rapid clip. She might have been nervous at his speed under the current conditions, but he drove with confident skill, so she decided to just close her eyes and continue praying.

He didn't speak until they had turned off the access road to the Western Sky and onto the main canyon road.

"Why didn't you tell me you were pregnant?"

Despite her fear, she bristled at the accusatory note in his voice. "Maybe because I didn't think it was any of your business."

"You made it my business when you showed up at my ranch, giving me some cock-and-bull story about needing a place to stay for a few days. Dammit, Mimi. If I'd known you were pregnant, I never would have worked you so hard."

She stared at him, her mouth open. Mimi. He'd called her Mimi.

"I thought it was a joke," he said, his voice disgusted. "Some funny story I could tell my men when I went back to my unit. Mimi Van Hoyt scrubbing my cobwebs and painting my spare bedroom."

"I'm not…"

"Cut the crap. We both know who you are."

A muscle flexed in his jaw and his eyes blazed and she gauged suddenly that he was furious with her.

"You…knew all along?"

"Of course I knew! I'm not an idiot, despite what

you apparently think. And yeah, I might have been living in a cave in the desert on and off for the last few years, but you were a little hard to miss whenever I did resurface."

She thought of all her ridiculous efforts to conceal her identity, all the half-truths and the outright prevarications, and her face burned with embarrassment. All for nothing. He had known, probably from the moment she crashed her car.

What must he have thought of her?

That didn't matter, she reminded herself. The important thing right now was doing all she could to save her baby.

"Why all the subterfuge?" he asked. "Why not just call one of your father's people to rescue you the minute you woke up after your accident and found yourself on the ranch? Instead, just about the first words out of your mouth were lies and they just kept coming."

She let out a breath. "You wouldn't understand."

"Not if you don't explain to me, *Maura*."

She made a face at his deliberate emphasis on the false name she'd given him. "Haven't you ever wanted to be someone else for a while? Maura Howard is safe. Ordinary. Just a nice woman living her nice comfortable life in anonymity. She hasn't made a total disaster of her life."

She hadn't meant to add that last part but it seemed particularly appropriate right now as she fought to save her baby.

"Why here? Why were you running to Gwen?"

"I needed a place away from the limelight for a while and the idea of escaping to Gwen's just felt right. I only found out myself about the baby the day before I arrived and I needed time to…come to terms with everything."

"So you decided to pretend to be someone else and worm your way into letting you me stay at the ranch."

That just about summed it out. "Yes," she admitted. "But whether I'm Mimi or Maura doesn't matter. I don't want to lose my baby."

"I'll do what I can to make sure you don't," he said.

Though he still seemed angry with her, after a long moment, he reached across the cab of the old pickup and folded her hand inside his much larger one.

Despite everything, her embarrassment and her anger that he had let her dig herself into a deeper hole of lies, she felt immensely comforted by the solid, corporeal reassurance of her hand in his.

He couldn't remember a more white-knuckle driving experience, counting the times he'd had to drive a Humvee down a precarious cliffside goat trail in the pitch-black wearing night-vision goggles that cut his peripheral view to nothing.

The road in Cold Creek Canyon had been plowed but was still icy and dangerous around the curves.

He could handle the road conditions. He'd been driving in snow since he was fourteen. But he'd never driven through snow with this abject fear in his gut. Every time Mimi caught her breath beside him at a bump or a sharp turn in the road, he wanted to just pull over and call for heli transport to take her to the nearest level-one trauma center, five hours away in Salt Lake City.

Though he knew he needed to keep both hands on the wheel because of the driving conditions—and he did for the most part—every once in a while he could sense her panic and fear start to break through her tight control and he couldn't resist reaching over and squeezing her fingers.

"Hang in there. We're almost there," he said.

She gave him a grateful look as she clung tight to his fingers.

By the time he reached the small medical clinic in Pine Gulch, his shoulders were knotted and he ached all over as if he had just finished hauling seventy pounds of gear on a fifty-mile march.

The parking lot and sidewalks of the clinic had been plowed already, he was relieved to see. Brant parked the truck near the entrance then hurried around to Mimi's side and scooped her out.

"I can walk," she murmured.

"Shut up and let me do this," he snapped, not at all in the mood to argue with her.

She raised an eyebrow but said nothing as he carefully made his way to the double front doors. Before he could thrust them open, Maggie Cruz Dalton appeared, pushing an empty wheelchair.

"I was watching for you," Maggie said, her features so calm and serene that a little of his panic naturally ebbed away.

She smiled at them both, though her attention was mostly fixed on Mimi, as he set her into the wheelchair. "I'm Maggie Dalton, Ms. Van Hoyt. My husband, Jake, is the town doctor and he'll be in to look at you as soon as we get you settled in an exam room."

Mimi shot Brant an accusing look as Maggie used her name instead of the whole Maura Howard alias, but he merely shrugged.

He wouldn't let her make him feel guilty for telling the Daltons the truth. He had called Maggie back when he went to get the pickup truck, after it occurred to him it was only fair and right to warn them their impending patient might require somewhat complicated security measures.

"We've cleared the waiting area and we'll get you back into an exam room right away," Maggie said.

"I… Thank you."

Mimi looked a little bit lost and a whole lot over-whelmed and he fought the urge to haul her back into his arms and promise her everything would be okay.

He was way, way out of his depth in this whole situation and felt completely inept and very male. If he had his preference, he would head over to The Bandito for a stiff drink while he waited, but he didn't think mentioning that right about now would earn him points with either Maggie or Mimi.

"I'll, um, just hang out here," Brant said.

He tried to pull his hand free from Mimi's grasp but she wouldn't let go and they tussled a little as Maggie pushed her down the hall toward an exam room.

"Would you feel better if you had someone familiar with you?" Maggie asked.

"Yes," Mimi admitted softly.

No, Brant wanted to say, horrified. *Hell* no.

But how could he just walk away when she apparently was in desperate need of a friendly face. "Do you want me to stay with you?" He voiced the obvious.

"You don't have to," she said in a small voice, and he sighed, giving up the liquor fantasy altogether.

"Sure, if that would make you feel better."

He was uncomfortably aware of the speculative glances Maggie was sending him. He glared at her, dreading the interrogation in store for him after all this.

He'd always had a tender spot in his heart for Magdalena Cruz Dalton, in part because of the courage she had shown when, as a former Army nurse, she had been injured in a bomb blast in the Middle East and lost her leg below the knee.

He had never seen her in action in her capacity as a nurse and he had to admit he was even more impressed when he witnessed her calming demeanor toward Mimi.

At the exam room, she turned to him. "Brant, please wait here in the hall while I help our patient change into a gown and get her settled."

How about the waiting room? Or the parking lot? Or back at the Western Sky?

"Sure," he said instead.

He leaned against the wall and was thinking how surreal this all was, when Maggie came out of the room a few moments later, closing the door behind her.

"You can go back in now."

"Do I have to?" he muttered, and she gave him a long look.

"You don't have to answer because it's none of my business. But I have to ask. Just out of curiosity, how on earth did Mimi Van Hoyt come to be threatening a miscarriage at the Western Sky?"

"It's a long story."

"And a fascinating one, I'm sure."

He sighed. "She's a friend of Gwen's, apparently, and she didn't know Gwen was in Europe. She came out to see her and ended up with me instead."

"So you're not the father."

He glared. "No! I just met the woman three days ago. I only gave her a place to stay while we waited out the storm."

"I'm guessing there's more to the story than that."

"No." *Except I've held her and kissed her until I couldn't see straight.* "Really, I barely know her."

"Be that as it may, it looks like you're her only support right now since Gwen's out of the country. It's good she has someone."

He would rather that someone be any other soul on earth except him, but Brant was determined to do his best to help her. He owed her, especially since it was his fault she was in that exam room right now. If he hadn't gone along with her deception—if he had admitted from the first day that he knew who she was instead of finding unexpected humor in watching her pretend to be someone else—she would not be in this situation. She would have been at one of the high-priced hotels in Jackson Hole sipping lattes in her fluffy pink designer boots instead of hanging curtains and falling off ladders in his spare bedroom.

His fault. He sighed. Just one more thing for which he bore responsibility. He had a feeling that one of these days the weight of all the guilt piled on top of him just might bury him.

Through the next twenty minutes, Mimi didn't let go of his hand. She clung to him while Maggie drew blood and checked her blood pressure. She wouldn't even let him leave when Jake Dalton came in to do an exam, though he was at least allowed to wait behind a little curtain near her head and away from the action, wishing like hell he was somewhere else.

When Jake was finished, he had Maggie hook a band with a monitor on it across Mimi's stomach and a moment later, a steady pulsing sound filled the exam room.

At the sound, the tension seemed to whoosh out of Mimi like a surveillance balloon shot through with mortar fire.

"That's the heartbeat, right?" she said, her famous green eyes bright with excitement and wonder and the echo of her fear.

"That's the heartbeat." Jake Dalton smiled at her, that winsome smile he shared with his two brothers, the one that managed to charm just about any woman in view of it. Mimi didn't seem to be an exception. Since the moment the Pine Gulch physician had come into the exam room, she had visibly relaxed, as if Jake could make everything right again.

Brant supposed that was a good technique for a doctor, to be able to inspire such trust in his patients.

"I'm happy to report that, despite your cramping, the heartbeat sounds strong and healthy," Jake said.

Mimi made a sound of relief mingled with a little sob and tightened her hand on Brant's. He squeezed back, wondering again how the real Mimi could seem so very different from her flighty, ditzy public persona.

"If it's all right with you," Jake went on, "I'd still like to do an ultrasound to get a little better look and check everything out."

"Whatever you think best."

"I can wait outside if you want," Brant offered.

She shook her head. "I'd like you to come," she said. "If you don't mind."

"Sure," he answered. What else could he say?

So he sat beside her while Jake covered her stomach with gel and then moved the ultrasound sensor over her. Brant couldn't seem to move his gaze from the monitor and the various mysterious shapes there, intrigued despite himself by the process and by that little alien-looking shape with a big head and tiny fingers.

Mimi looked enthralled. "Can you tell what it is?" she asked.

"Not yet. A few more weeks," Jake replied. After a few more moments, he set down the wand and handed her a huge pile of paper towels to wipe off all the goop. "You haven't miscarried, despite the cramping. I can't say it's not still a possibility, but right now your baby is alive and appears to be healthy."

Mimi exhaled a long breath and squeezed Brant's fingers. "Oh, thank you, Dr. Dalton. Thank you so much."

Jake smiled. "I didn't do anything but check things out. I want you to come back immediately if you have more cramping or spotting."

"Of course."

"And I don't know what your travel plans are, but I would feel better if you stay put for now. In fact, I would recommend limited bed rest for at least a few days. That means you can get up to move from room to room, but not much more than that. Can you swing that?"

She pulled her hand away and didn't look at Brant. "I don't… It's not right for me to impose on Major Western more than I already have. Perhaps I could check into a motel in the area."

Brant frowned. "Stop right there. You're staying at the Western Sky."

He was invested in this now. No way was he going to sit by and let her fight to save her baby without him.

"When do you have to report back?" Maggie asked him.

"My flight leaves Tuesday." He could request an additional few days of emergency leave but he and Maggie both knew he wouldn't get it, not for these circumstances.

"She can stay with me until I have to take off," he said. "If she still needs bed rest after that, she can stay with Easton at Winder Ranch."

For some strange reason, Mimi didn't look exactly thrilled at that idea, which he found odd. Everybody liked Easton.

"Or with us," Maggie said. "We've got plenty of room. Don't worry, we'll find a place for you, Ms. Van Hoyt."

"Thank you," she said, with a fairly good rendition of her usual radiant smile.

She hadn't moved her slim hands from her abdomen since he'd found her standing so frightened and pale on the front porch. By all appearances, it looked as if Mimi was excited about this baby.

Who was the father? he wondered, trying to rack his brain to see if he had remembered seeing her with some special date in the tabloids lately. He hadn't paid enough attention to really care but now he wanted to run over to the grocery store and buy every copy of the gossip rags off the stands.

One kiss, no matter how earthshaking, didn't give him the right to be jealous, he reminded himself.

"Just take it easy, eat healthy foods and drink plenty

of fluids," Jake was saying. "I'd like to see you again on Friday. I'll see if I can swing out to the Western Sky."

"Thank you. Both of you," she said to the doctor as he and Maggie headed out of the room. Brant rose to leave with them in order to give her privacy to dress, but he didn't move away from the exam table as a new thought occurred to him.

"Do you need help getting dressed? I can send Maggie back in."

"I think I can handle it. Thank you." She paused and, just before he reached the door, she gripped his fingers again. "Thank you so much for everything, Brant. I don't know what I would have done if you hadn't been here with me."

She wouldn't have been hurt in the first place if not for him.

"You would have been fine. I think you're tougher than you think, Mimi."

"I'm not," she said, but as he left, he thought she looked intrigued at the idea.

Tough or not, Mimi must have been completely exhausted from the stress of the afternoon. By the time he drove the short distance from the clinic to the mouth of Cold Creek Canyon, she was asleep, curled up beside him with her cheek resting against the worn upholstery.

Even though the return trip to the ranch lacked the urgency that had pushed him so hard to drive a little faster than conditions warranted on the way to town, the drive home seemed shorter somehow. Maybe because his stomach wasn't a knot of nerves this time.

At twilight, the canyon seemed spectacularly beautiful, with the mountains looming in the distance and the dark shadows of the Douglas fir a bold contrast to the pure, blinding white of the snow.

When he passed Hope Springs, he saw Nate Cavazos clearing snow from his neighbor's driveway with his tractor, headlights beaming. He lifted a hand in the customary wave and Nate smiled and waved back.

He loved that about Pine Gulch. That sense of community, of being part of something bigger. Shoveling out your neighbor's driveway, casseroles and chicken soup on your doorstep when you were sick, helping anybody in need just because you can.

He remembered when Curtis drowned, the outpouring of support for his parents. Some of the men in town had helped his dad put in his crops that year when he'd been too stunned to do it, then had been there throughout the haying season to help him cut and bale when he was too drunk to bring in his own crop.

It had been that same sense of community, he supposed, that had impelled Guff Winder to keep an eye out for his neighbor's son and then to step in and take care of business when he saw things weren't right.

Maybe that's why he was so conflicted about selling the ranch. He loved it here and found something deeply compelling about being tied to a place, something that wasn't just about geography.

Would he lose that if he sold the ranch?

He would always be connected to Pine Gulch and Cold Creek Canyon through Easton. She and Quinn and Cisco were his family, all he had, and nothing would ever change that. But he had to admit that Easton was right. If he sold the ranch, nothing would be the same.

When he reached the house, he turned off the engine of the big truck and glanced in the fading light at his passenger.

He wasn't crazy about this protective mode that seemed to take over him when he was around her, something that made no rational sense.

Why should he feel any sense of obligation toward the woman? She had more money and resources at her disposal than he could even imagine, enough to probably contract a small private army of her own.

She probably had a dozen houses around the world where she could be recuperating right now. Paris. London. New York. So why was she determined to hide out in Podunk eastern Idaho with him?

Was she escaping her father? The baby's father? The paparazzi? Or all of the above?

Whatever it was, he knew damn well he ought to just let her deal with her own troubles. But at this point, he knew it was far too late for him to step back.

"Mimi, we're home," he said, after allowing himself only a few more moments' indulgence to just look at her.

Her big, long-lashed green eyes blinked sleepily at him as she hovered on the edge of consciousness.

"I'm…sorry," she said with a yawn. "I fell asleep. How rude of me."

"To sleep when your body demanded it? That's not rude. If there's one thing any soldier understands, it's the value of sleeping whenever you can steal the chance."

He moved around the truck and opened the door for her. "Come on, let's get you inside," he said as he scooped her small, curvy weight into his arms.

"You don't have to carry me," she protested. "Dr. Dalton never said I couldn't walk."

He ignored her objection—just as he tried to ignore how warm and feminine and sweet smelling she was in his arms.

"I would hate for you to fall out here. It's still slick."

"What if *you* fall?"

He knew he shouldn't enjoy the way her body slid against his chest when he shrugged. "Then I'll figure out how to hit the ground first so I spare you the brunt of it."

"Could you really do that?"

He smiled a little at the disbelief in her eyes. "I have no idea. But since I'm not going to slip, we won't have to find out, will we?"

For some reason she was staring at his mouth and his smile slid away.

"Don't stop," she murmured.

"I'm only opening the door," he said. "I was planning to set you down on the sofa in the family room by the fire."

"I meant, don't stop smiling. You're far less terrifying when you smile."

Terrifying? She was afraid of him? After he had just spent a deeply uncomfortable afternoon holding her hand in a doctor's office?

His gaze met hers and suddenly he remembered the kiss between them, the softness of her mouth and the way her hands had curled into his hair and the sweet, sexy sounds she made when his mouth found hers.

She was the first to look away. "The sofa would be a good place to set me, but the, um, powder room would actually be better."

He set her down outside the door of the bathroom

just off the kitchen. "I imagine Simone's going to need to go out. I'll take care of that and then build up the fire in the woodstove again."

"Thank you." To his discomfort, she reached up and brushed her fingers on his cheek. "Thank you for everything. I'm really sorry I dragged you into this."

"You wouldn't have been hurt if not for me," he said in a low voice.

She dropped her hand and gazed at him in surprise. "What do you mean?"

"If I had admitted from the first that I knew who you were, you never would have been up on that ladder."

"This was *not* your fault, Brant. If anyone's to blame, I am. I lied to you and used you, only because I needed a place to stay for a few days and the Western Sky was convenient for my needs. I selfishly didn't think for one minute about you only having a few days of peace to yourself. I never considered you might have better things to do with your brief free time than entertaining me."

She looked sad suddenly, as bereft as she had on the way to the clinic when she had been in fear for her child.

"That's who I am," she said in a low voice. "Selfish, irresponsible Mimi Van Hoyt, who never thinks of anyone but herself. So now you know."

She closed the door between them firmly before he could reply. A few days ago, he would have agreed. But right now, Brant didn't know what to believe.

Chapter Eight

"Oh!" Mimi exclaimed four hours later. "You are nothing but a dirty, rotten cheater!"

The louse in question raised an eyebrow. "Hey, I won that hand fair and square. Is it my fault you're a lousy poker player?"

"Oh!" Mimi grabbed a kernel of popcorn from the bowl beside her and tossed it at him. To her regret, it hit his chest and bounced off again. "Who ever would have guessed that the upright, honorable Major Brant Western cheats at cards?"

"I did *not* cheat." He gave her a long look, that sexy mouth of his tilted slightly at one corner. "I could have, about a dozen times when you weren't paying attention, but I opted to claim higher ground."

She sniffed at this with a dismissive gesture at the pile of toothpicks in front of him. Compared to her very tiny winnings, his stash of toothpicks looked like a beaver dam.

"When you asked me if I wanted to play five-card stud, it might have been fair for you to mention you're as relentless as an Atlantic City card shark."

"You mean I forgot to mention the three years I spent on the pro poker circuit?"

"I believe it. I'm curious, though. How did you fit the poker circuit in between deployments."

"It wasn't easy but I managed."

She shook her head at his teasing, though she had to admit she loved this lighthearted side of him. Except for those few dark moments after they returned from the clinic when he tried to shoulder the blame for her threatened miscarriage, he had seemed like a different man throughout the evening.

Every now and again she had seen a certain brooding look in his eyes but he took pains to keep everything between them light and easy.

"I'm just about down to my last toothpick so I guess that means you've cleaned me out," she said.

"I might be persuaded to stake you a little more if you want to keep going," he said.

"And end up having my kneecaps broken by your little toothpick loan sharks? I don't think so, Major."

He laughed a low, rich laugh she was quickly coming to adore.

He was doing his best to keep her mind off her lingering worry by distraction. So far it had been a remarkably effective strategy. Not perfect, but nearly so.

"Who taught you to play poker so well?" she asked him. "Did you learn from your Army buddies?"

He shook his head with a grin. "That would be Cisco.

He never met a game of chance he didn't like. Craps, dice, whatever. Our favorite game was called Bull, er, shoot. Have you played it?"

"Is that where you hold a card faceup on your forehead and no one can see his own card but you can see what everyone else has?"

He smiled. "Nope. That one is called Guts. The game I'm talking about is also called Cheat."

"Oh, that's appropriate. I can see why you liked it."

He gave her a mock glare. "I didn't cheat! Tonight, anyway. But the whole object of Cheat is to lie your way through. You deal the whole deck and then you take turns with every player discarding all their cards by rank in order from aces down. Whether you really have that number of cards or not, you BS your way through. Too bad it doesn't work very well with only two people. Cisco, Quinn, Easton and I would play for hours. Cisco could beat all of us, just about every time."

She adjusted to a more comfortable position on the sofa. "Why's that?"

"Well, Quinn was always too busy trying to count the cards so he could figure out who was lying and Easton had some really obvious tells. She would tug the ends of her hair when she was trying to bull us. To this day, she doesn't realize she does it."

Easton again. She swallowed her frown. She was growing tired of the other woman's name. "You must all have been good friends."

He shuffled the cards with great dexterity. "We were more than friends. I guess you could say we were more like brothers, or the closest thing to it."

"Easton's not a boy." She had to point out the obvious.

He smiled. "No, but she thought she was. She was a

real tomboy and loved to follow us around. We didn't mind. She was a cute kid."

"The others—Cisco and Quinn—did they live close by?"

"Sort of." He was quiet for a long moment. "We all lived together at a ranch just down the canyon. Winder Ranch. We were in foster care there."

"Foster care?" She forgot all about the cards and her hands tightened so much on Simone that the dog jumped off her lap in a huff and moved to Brant's lap. "But you told me you grew up here."

"I said I lived here for the most part. That means until I was twelve. Then the neighbors took me in because of…problems here."

"Problems?"

He looked as if he regretted saying anything. "I told you about my brother dying. Nothing was the same after that. My parents both drank afterward and then my mom ran off and things got worse. I guess you could say things around here hit rock bottom and a neighbor couple took me in. They already had one foster son, Quinn Southerland. I was only there a few months before they found Cisco Del Norte living by himself in a stolen tent in the mountains after his dad died. After that, we were inseparable. The Four Winds, Jo called us, because of our names."

"Southerland, Del Norte, Western. Easton's the fourth?"

He smiled, even after Simone did her favorite little lap-hopping thing and jumped onto him. "Right. She was the Winders' niece who lived on the ranch with her parents since her dad was foreman. She was more like a little sister to us. Still is."

Sister. He considered Easton a sister.

"She's not your girlfriend, then?"

"Easton? No way!" He was quiet for a moment. "Truth is, I've always suspected she and Cisco have feelings for each other but neither of them has ever said anything about it and I don't want to go there."

Mimi suddenly decided she liked the other woman much better.

"The four of us got into so much trouble," he went on. "You wouldn't believe it. Sneaking out for midnight fishing trips into the mountains, taking the horses when we weren't supposed to, playing pranks on the homecoming dance committee."

"You hellions."

He flashed her a wry look. "We were. Though I will say, I usually tried to be the voice of reason and managed to talk the others out of almost everything immoral or illegal."

"So you were the boring one," she teased.

"True enough." He paused. "I probably tried a little too hard to be perfect so Jo and Guff wouldn't have any reason to change their minds about giving me a home."

Her heart ached for the boy he must have been. "But you didn't want to be perfect, did you?"

Her guess surprised another laugh out of him. "No. I wanted to be like Cisco. He wasn't afraid of anything. He could talk his way out of just about any kind of trouble that came along. Still can, for that matter."

"Does he live around here?"

His eyes clouded a little. "No. He hasn't since he was eighteen. He's in Latin America somewhere."

"What does he do there?"

"He's pretty closemouthed about it. I have a few

guesses but I don't know for sure. To be honest, I'm not sure I want to know."

"Something illegal or immoral?"

"Possibly," he said, with wariness in his voice, and she didn't press him.

"And the other one? Southerland?"

"Quinn." He smiled with genuine affection. "Right now he's in Costa Rica on his honeymoon. Remember, we were talking about his wedding the other day with Easton? He married a girl we knew in high school, Tess Jamison. She's actually expecting a baby, too."

He made a face. "Sorry, I didn't mean to run on. I imagine life around here must seem pretty provincial compared to private Swiss boarding school and holidays in Monaco."

She sipped at the hot cocoa he'd brought her earlier, which was now, unfortunately, lukewarm. "The boarding school was outside Paris, actually, and we generally summered in Cannes."

"A far cry from Pine Gulch, Idaho. You must be bored to tears playing five-card stud and listening to my meanderings down memory lane."

"Not at all," she admitted. "If you want to know the truth, I've been thinking how lucky you are."

"Lucky?" He looked astonished. "Because my brother died and my mom ran off and my dad was a drunk who liked to use his fists a little too much on his surviving kid?"

"Not about that. That part is horrible."

She couldn't imagine it, actually. Though her father had been arrogant and distant, she'd never worried he would physically hurt her.

"I just meant this place. Cold Creek. There's a serenity here. I can't explain it. And you had all these people you love to share it with."

"You didn't have anyone?"

She shifted restlessly on the sofa. "Of course. I refuse to play the poor little rich girl card. I had a life of privilege beyond what most people can even imagine. I know that. Yachts. Penthouse apartments. Private jets. I hate to admit this, but I didn't fly a commercial airplane until the first time I snuck out of boarding school when I was nine, after I bought my own plane ticket back to New York out of my allowance."

"You flew by yourself from Paris to New York when you were nine?"

She shrugged. "It was the Christmas holidays and I wanted nothing more than to be home. My father was newly married again. Number four, I think. Jemma, the wife before Gwen—and they were expecting a baby right after Christmas and they didn't want me there in the middle of the happy event. Turns out my half brother Jack was born on Christmas Eve, just a few hours before I showed up at our apartment in the city. My father wasn't pleased to see me. Neither was Jemma, needless to say, but I adored Jack. Still do, for that matter. Of all the half and stepsiblings, he's my favorite."

She smiled a little, thinking of her half brother. He had inherited his mother's looks and their father's brain, a formidable combination.

He was going to be a wonderful uncle to her baby, if Jemma let him see Mimi. But then, he was almost eighteen and his mother wouldn't have much of a choice in the matter.

"You said the wife before Gwen. She was your step-mother? Why didn't she ever say anything?" He looked rather dazed at the idea.

"Gwen considered her brief marriage a huge mistake. She was the only one of my father's wives who voluntarily left him. He dumped all the others."

"Nice."

"If Jack is my favorite sibling, Gwen is my favorite ex-stepmother."

"How many do you have?"

She had to think about it. "Four exes and one current, who at least has longevity. Marta has been married to Werner for going on eight years, which is something of a record for him."

"What about your mother?"

"She died when I was three. I barely remember her. I'd like to think she was the love of his life and he married all the others to assuage his broken heart. But then, I'd like to believe strawberry cheesecake isn't really fattening, either."

She was quiet for a moment. The only sounds in the room were Simone's snuffly breathing on his lap and the low crackling of the fire in the stove.

"None of them was horrible, Cinderella-grade stepmother material or anything, but they mostly just tolerated me. Gwen was the best. She never once made me feel like I was in the way."

"In contrast to your father."

She looked away from that perceptive blue-eyed gaze. "I never said that."

"You didn't have to say it. I'm good at picking up on the unspoken. It's a handy skill when you're dealing with military command."

"Well, I'm afraid you missed the target here by a mile, soldier."

"Did I?"

She made a big production of arranging the throw over her feet as she mulled how to answer him. Lying seemed silly, suddenly, when he already knew more about her than anyone else.

She had been raised to be cautious of talking about herself. After several so-called friends had turned out to be tipping off the paparazzi to her every move, Mimi had a tough time trusting people.

But somehow she knew Brant would never sell her out to the tabloids. He was a good man. If she had any doubt about that, he had proved his worth today at the clinic when he had sat by her side the entire time, despite his obvious discomfort.

She didn't know how she would ever repay him for that kindness.

"What do you know about Werner Van Hoyt?" she asked.

"Not much, really. Only that he's a brilliant real estate investor and the force behind most of the movers and shakers in Hollywood."

"He's also abrasive and overbearing and treats everyone in his life from his current wife to his various children to the damn pool boy with that same detached indifference, as if we were all interchangeable cuff links."

"And so you compensate by jumping from scandal to scandal in the hopes that you can ruffle his calm a little and make him notice that one of his cuff links doesn't quite match."

She had a wild urge to pull the blanket over her head to protect her psyche from that steady gaze of his.

"Aren't you the smart one?" she finally said. "It took me three years on a therapist's couch to pick that up."

"I've only known you a few days," he said, "but I think you're smarter than you let the world see."

She flashed him a look under her lashes, wondering if he was being sarcastic, but he only continued watching her steadily.

"About some things," she muttered. "Relationships, not so much. I'm pretty stupid about those."

He leaned back. "Does the little squirt's father fit in that *stupid* category?"

"He's right at the top of the list." She sighed, knowing she was going to have to tell him, if not all the truth, at least some of it. He deserved that much for standing by her all day.

"The baby's father won't be in the picture. He's… unavailable."

"Married?"

"Not yet, but soon. That doesn't make it better, I know."

He continued watching her steadily, and she traced a finger along the fringed edge of the afghan, avoiding his gaze. "When I told him I was pregnant, he automatically assumed I would take care of the *little problem,* as he termed it, so he could continue on with his big plans to live happily ever after with someone else. He was not very happy when I told him I wanted to keep the baby."

He was quiet for a long moment. "He's the stupid son of a bitch, then, not you."

She laughed a little but then saw by the hardness of his jaw that he was completely serious and something warm and sweet fluttered through her.

"He is. And you know what, he doesn't matter."

He didn't, she realized. Somehow, today, amidst her frantic fear for the child, Marco's harsh words, his fury with her, had become completely unimportant. Her priorities had shifted and rearranged themselves and now all she wanted was for her baby to be healthy.

"I want this baby. And I'm going to be a darn good mother."

He smiled. "I don't doubt it for a minute."

His words soaked through her like spring rains on a parched desert. She hadn't realized how desperately she had needed someone to believe in her until Brant spoke but she suddenly felt tears prickle behind her eyes.

"Hey. Don't cry."

"I'm sorry. It's just…been quite a day."

Before she realized what he intended, he moved beside her on the couch and pulled her into his arms. "You've been a trooper, Mimi. You've been strong and courageous and done everything the doc told you to do. You're going to be a wonderful mother."

He kissed her, something she sensed he meant only as a gesture of affection and maybe respect.

But as his mouth touched hers, firm and strong, she was astonished as tenderness surged through her. She felt surrounded by him, safe and warm and comforted, somehow.

She tightened her arms around his neck, eyes closed as she memorized the scent of him, masculine and enticing. She didn't want to move from this place. She wanted to stay right here beside him feeling each breath against her skin, with the heat of him soaking through her and this fragile tenderness taking root in the empty corners of her heart.

Eventually he pulled away, looking slightly dazed. "You need your rest. Come on, I'll help you to your room."

He would have carried her again but she insisted on walking.

"I'll put Simone out one last time and then bring her to you when she's ready to settle down," he said when they reached her door.

"Thank you."

"Good night, Mimi." He pressed his lips to her forehead again and she felt something dangerous shift and slide inside her heart.

After she closed the door, she leaned against it, her thoughts tangled.

She was in serious trouble here. Once on holiday in Sicily she had climbed Mount Etna and had stood teetering on the edge, her nerves jangling and her heart racing.

She felt exactly like that right now, as if she stood peering into the abyss. She was in grave danger of falling for Brant, tumbling headlong into love with a tall, serious Army Ranger with solemn eyes and a deep core of decency. She had thought herself in love before, but all those other emotions paled in comparison to what she feared she could feel for Brant.

She couldn't love him. Whatever it took, she had to protect her heart. Right now her focus had to be her baby. She couldn't afford to waste her energy and time on a man who was unsuitable and unavailable.

No matter how much she might want him.

Chapter Nine

He had to get the hell out of here.

Two days after Mimi fell off the ladder, Brant stirred the coals in the woodstove, then tossed another log on the red embers.

Behind him, he could hear another Alfred Hitchcock movie starting on the movie channel they'd been watching all day and he closed his eyes, not sure if he was man enough to endure the temptation of sitting beside Mimi for another two hours, with her sweet, delicate scent teasing his senses and her famous green eyes sparkling brightly and her wide smile clutching at his heart.

For two days, they had played games, had laughed at Simone's antics, had pored through the stack of baby books Mimi had squirreled away in her stacks of luggage.

This morning, one of the movie channels was having

a Hitchcock marathon. They had watched *The Birds* and *Psycho* and next up was *Vertigo*. He wasn't sure he was up for that one, since he was entirely too dizzy around her as it was.

He had been very careful not to kiss her again, fearful that once he started he wouldn't be able to stop.

He needed a little distance from her or he was very much afraid he would find himself slipping headfirst down some dangerous slope with her and be unable to clamber back to safe ground.

The trouble was, he didn't want to leave. He loved her company. Mimi was clever and fun and wholeheartedly embraced everything she did, whether that was playing Monopoly or throwing a toy for her dog or curling up, completely engrossed in an old movie.

Before he'd come to know her these past few days, he might have expected the tabloid version of Mimi Van Hoyt to be petulant and resentful at her enforced inactivity. He could easily have envisioned temper tantrums and hysterics.

Instead, she was sweet and funny and showed a surprising gratitude toward everything he did, whether it was handing her another pillow or bringing her a grilled cheese sandwich and bowl of canned soup for lunch or just putting her little furball outside when Simone had to take care of business.

He was entirely too drawn to this Mimi and for the first time he could remember, he wasn't looking forward to returning to duty. If he could have dragged this time out longer, he would have tried to figure out a way, but he knew he only had three days left here before he flew out.

He only needed a little perspective, he thought. He had spent just about every waking moment of the last two days with Mimi. Once he was away from her, he would be able to shift his priorities where they should be. The Army had been his life since he was eighteen years old, and a few magical days with a beautiful woman couldn't shake that.

Through the glass door of the woodstove, he watched the flames lick at the log and Brant decided this would be a good time to escape, while the opening credits of the next movie had just started to roll.

"Go ahead and watch this one without me. I'm going to go feed the animals and check on Gwen's place, then I'll come back inside and fix some dinner for us."

Mimi didn't answer him and he turned around to find she was asleep, her long dark lashes fanning those high cheekbones and one arm tucked around Simone, who was curled up beside her on the sofa.

The little white bichon frise opened one black eye when she felt Brant's scrutiny and he could swear she grinned at him.

Yeah, he figured he'd be grinning, too, if he were snuggled up against all that warmth and softness.

One of Mimi's dark curls had drifted across her cheek and he reached a hand to push it out of the way, then froze, his hand extended.

He had to get out of here. Now, before he did something inordinately stupid like sit down beside her, pull her against him and wake her by kissing that delectable mouth. He had to go, even if that only meant escaping to the barn for a while.

Leaving the television buzzing softly, he moved with as much stealth as he could muster to the mudroom off the kitchen, where his winter gear hung.

A few moments later, he was outside in the icy air.

The sun was setting in a blaze of orange and purple and the ranch glowed with that particularly beautiful slant of winter light that turned everything rosy and soft.

When he reached the barn, he turned back to look at the ranch house, sprawling and unpretentious in the sunset.

Even in the worst years, when his family life had been in tatters, he had loved the house and the ranch, with the creek running just a short distance away and the mountains a solid, reassuring presence in the background.

He had dreaded coming home during those years when his father had turned cruel and bitter but he had never blamed the ranch for that. Even in the worst of it, he still hadn't wanted to leave. Guff Winder practically had to drag him away and those first few months at Winder Ranch he had cried himself to sleep just about every night after Quinn was asleep in the room they'd shared.

Eventually he had settled into the routine of life with the Winders and having an instant older brother and then Cisco a few months later. The six years he spent at Winder Ranch were the most peaceful of his life.

Peace.

He remembered Mimi saying she felt peace and serenity at the ranch. As he gazed at his home, he realized that was the indefinable emotion that seeped through him when he was with her.

She soothed him, in a way he couldn't explain. He let out a long breath. That made absolutely no sense but here in the pure clarity of dusk, he didn't see how he could deny it.

He had come home for leave with an aching heart, guilty and grieving at his own failures that had cost good men their lives. He knew he would always regret the ambush, that he hadn't trusted his instincts that something was wrong, but these days with Mimi had distracted him from brooding over it. When he was with her, he could release the pain of regret for a little while and focus on the gift of the moment.

He sighed. What good was it to get away from her physically by coming outside if he couldn't shake her from his mind? With renewed determination, he headed into the barn, resolved to focus on the mundane for a while.

An hour later, he had finished the regular chores and was busy at the woodpile, replenishing Gwen's supply of split logs, when he heard the sound of a vehicle approaching the house.

Easton had said she would stop by sometime tonight or tomorrow. Assuming it was her, he set the split log carefully on the stack, then headed around the corner of the house just in time to find Jake Dalton holding open the passenger door of an SUV and reaching inside to help his wife climb out.

The tenderness of Jake's concern for Maggie warmed Brant. She deserved a safe haven after the hell she'd been through and it looked as if she had found it.

He reached them just before they headed up the stairs. "Hey, Doc. Maggie," he said with a smile.

"Hey, you." Maggie smiled back. "How's our patient?"

"She's had a pretty calm time the last few days. No more cramps. She was sleeping when I came outside an hour ago."

"Just what she needs to be doing," Jake said. "I'll go check on her, if you don't mind."

"Go ahead," Brant said.

Before Jake went inside, he sent Maggie a look loaded with meaning that flew right past Brant.

"Come on inside," he said. "Do you need help up the stairs?"

She shook her head. "I get around pretty well these days. Stairs don't bug me nearly as much as they used to."

To prove the truth of her words, she moved up the porch steps with smooth, easy movements.

Inside, he expected her to follow her husband immediately to Mimi, but she grabbed his arm in the entryway.

"So Mimi's doing better. How about you?"

He flashed her a searching look, wondering at the concern in her eyes. "Fine. I'm not the patient here."

"Easton told me you've had a rough time in Afghanistan in the last month. That you lost some friends."

He sighed. He hadn't intended to say anything to anyone about the failed mission, but Easton had cornered him the night before the wedding and wiggled it out of him.

"Easton's got a big mouth."

"You know East. She worries about you. But she's not talking around town about you, I promise. She wouldn't have even mentioned it to me, I think, except we bumped into each other at the grocery store. I think she thought I might have some insight into the situation because of, well, my past. She was worried about you since you seemed more stoic than usual. Which is saying something, by the way."

He didn't want to talk about this right now, but he didn't know how to avoid it. He could understand why Easton would think Maggie had a special perspective on the situation after her own military experience and losing her leg in Afghanistan.

"I'm doing okay. Things have been…better the last few days." That was as close as he would come to admitting that Mimi had helped him, without even knowing it.

"What happened? She didn't know details."

"Ambush in a little village in the Paktika Province. I was supposed to meet a high-level contact who insisted on giving his information only to a high-ranking officer. We had intel that the village where the meet was supposed to take place was safe, so I picked twelve of my best men to come with me. The intel was wrong."

He had a memory flash of shouts and screams, civilians caught in the middle of what turned into an intense fight for their lives. "We drove straight into it. My team fought back but in the firefight, three good men died."

"Did you do anything wrong?" she finally asked.

He sighed. Trust Maggie to hit the heart of the matter. "Strategically and militarily, no. I followed protocol to the letter and we had duplicate intelligence that said the area had been cleared of insurgents and any IEDs. But I should have listened to my gut. My instincts were telling me the situation was off, that the contact wasn't trustworthy, and I ignored them."

Her features were soft with a compassion he didn't want to see right now. "And of course you're blaming yourself for the deaths of your men."

His throat felt tight but he ruthlessly crammed the emotions down. "Of course. Wouldn't you?"

She was silent for a long moment and then she reached between them and squeezed his hand. "My first month in Kabul, I cried myself to sleep every night, until you and Nate came to visit me. Do you remember that?"

"I do." He somehow managed a smile, though it wasn't easy. He and Nate Cavazos, a fellow Ranger and Pine Gulch native, hadn't been in the same company but both happened to be deployed in Afghanistan at the same time as Maggie and they'd been able to coordinate leave so they could all meet up a few times.

"Do you remember what you said to me? 'Mag, if being here doesn't scare the hell out of you, then something's wrong with your head.' And you told me only an idiot would be too afraid to talk to somebody when they were hurting or scared. I finally confessed to my commanding officer how terrified I was and he was able to say all the right things to help me through it. I never would have gone to him if you hadn't nudged me in that direction. So I'm going to throw your words back at you. Don't be an idiot, okay? I know you only have a few days before you head back, but if you need to talk, you know where I am."

"Right."

"Nate's here, too, you know. You could talk to him if you'd rather."

"Yeah, I drove past him the other day while he was shoveling snow out at the old Hirschi place but it was the day I brought Mimi to the clinic so I didn't have a chance to talk. How's he doing?"

Brant knew Nate's world had changed radically six months earlier when his sister and her husband had died, leaving him guardian of his two nieces. He'd left the military to take up his responsibilities and Brant had been meaning to catch up with him ever since.

"Did you know he's getting married?" Maggie asked.

"Really?"

"Yes, to a woman from Virginia who stayed at his guest ranch over Christmas."

"No kidding? I hadn't heard."

She grinned, looking very much like the girl he remembered from school. "Then you also don't know the truly juicy gossip."

"Do tell," he said dryly.

"Turns out his guest—and now his fiancée—is actually Hank Dalton's illegitimate daughter."

"Poor thing."

Just about everybody in Pine Gulch had hated Hank Dalton, Jake's father—Maggie most of all.

But instead of agreeing with him, she only smacked his shoulder. "Since Hank's been dead for years, Emery gets all the benefits of being a Dalton without having to ever deal with him. Wade, Jake and Seth are over the moon to have a sister after all these years. You should have seen them all yelling and carrying on when she and Nate came over with the girls on New Year's Eve to tell everyone."

"I'm sorry I missed that."

Instead of spending New Year's surrounded by neighbors and the scents of home, he had been in Afghanistan planning a mission that would end up taking his friends' lives.

Unexpectedly, as if sensing his train of thought, Maggie reached to give him a hug and he felt those emotions jumble together inside him all over again. "You'll be okay, Brant. Just give it time."

"Thanks, Mag."

"Anytime, Major." She stepped away. "Enough of that. Let's go see how your patient's doing."

As she walked toward the family room with barely

a limp, he thought he would like to have even a small portion of Maggie's courage and strength to face his own battles.

Dr. Dalton removed his stethoscope from her abdomen and pulled Mimi's sweater back down to cover her skin. "A strong and healthy heartbeat. I can't make any promises, but so far everything looks normal. Perfect, even. I have high hopes that you'll have an uneventful pregnancy from here on out."

A weight she hadn't realized had been pressing down on her heart for two days seemed to lift at his words.

"Oh, thank you. Thank you so much," she exclaimed just as the doctor's lovely dark-haired wife walked in with Brant.

Mimi wasn't really aware of doing it but she must have reached for Major Western's hand. He was at her side in an instant.

"Brant, Dr. Dalton says the baby still has a healthy heartbeat," she said. "For now, everything is okay with the pregnancy. Since I've had no more cramping, he thinks we might be past the immediate danger."

Relief washed across his clean-cut, handsome features. "That's wonderful news."

To her surprise, he hugged her and she returned the embrace, giddy joy bursting through her.

As she lifted her head, she caught a raised-eyebrow sort of look pass between Dr. Dalton and his wife. With considerable chagrin, she realized she and Brant were acting like more like a happy couple than the casual acquaintances they should have been.

Her heart ached with the knowledge that she didn't want to be only casual acquaintances with him, especially after these magical few days. She wanted so much more from him, even though she knew the dream was impossible.

She eased away from the embrace and forced herself to turn back to the physician. "I can't thank you enough for coming out to check on things. I thought house calls went the way of rotary phones and beehive hairdos."

"We're still a little old-fashioned here in Pine Gulch when necessary," Dr. Dalton said.

"Well, I'm very indebted to you both."

She didn't know how she would repay them but she would figure out a way. Perhaps a generous donation to their clinic so they could continue the practice Brant told her about of providing free or reduced care twice a month to patients without health insurance.

"Thank you," she repeated, though the words seemed woefully inadequate.

"I was just about to heat up some lasagna from the freezer for dinner if you two have time to stick around," Brant said.

"We can't," Maggie said regretfully. "The kids have been at Caroline and Wade's all afternoon playing with their cousins and we need to get them home. Thank you for the offer, though."

"You're welcome. Thanks for stopping by. I owe you," Brant said.

"Remember what I said," Maggie murmured to Brant, piquing Mimi's curiosity. "Don't be an idiot."

His mouth lifted in a small smile. "More than usual, you mean? I appreciate the advice, Mag."

She hugged him tightly then kissed his cheek. "If we don't see you again before you ship out, take care of yourself over there, Major."

"I'll do my best," he answered, then shook Dr. Dalton's hand before walking them to the door.

Everyone liked Brant, she realized. There was something so reassuring about him and that air of competence and quiet integrity about him. She wanted to just curl up against him and let him take care of all her troubles. Did others sense it, too?

"What was Maggie talking to you about so seriously?" she asked when he returned to the living room. "What did she think you were being an idiot about?"

That muscle worked in his jaw. "She thinks I'm on edge because of what happened to my men."

"Are you?"

"I'm fine," he said abruptly. "I'm going to go heat up the lasagna. I think I've got some rolls in the freezer. I'll grab some of those, too."

She didn't like the shuttered look on his features or the way he seemed so careful about avoiding her gaze, but if he preferred to confide in Maggie Dalton, Mimi couldn't do anything about it.

Dinner turned out to be an awkward affair, something she wouldn't have expected at all after the easy camaraderie they'd slipped into the past two days.

Brant was mostly silent, though he ate with the single-minded energy she had come to realize was probably characteristic of a battlefield warrior who wasn't certain when he would find his next meal.

After dinner, she played with Simone for a while, running through the little dog's limited bag of tricks. The dog seemed to have picked up on the tension between the two of them. She was restless, sniffing in all the corners of the room and insisting on going out three or four times until Brant finally picked her up and stood by the window, petting her and looking out into the night.

"Want to watch something?" Mimi asked. "Or you could give me a chance to win back my fortune in toothpicks."

He shook his head and returned to his window-gazing. When he finally turned back, his features were tight, his mouth a hard, implacable line.

She thought he was angry at something, until she saw his eyes and she had to catch her breath at the anguish there.

"I told you that a month ago three of my men were killed in a botched operation."

"Yes."

He let out a long breath, as if all the air in his lungs had turned sour. "I didn't tell you it was my fault they were killed."

"Oh, Brant. I'm sure that's not true. You were doing your job."

"I was. But I put them in that village. I ordered them there as my security detail. I should have sensed we were heading straight into an ambush."

She didn't know what to say, how to comfort him. What did she know about warriors and their demons? But she sensed he needed to talk and she could provide that, if nothing else.

"Maggie told me I should talk to someone about what I've been going through. She thinks that will help me work it out in my head. I want to just forget everything but…somehow it seems important that you know."

She held her breath as she heard the emotion behind

his words. He was not a man who leaned on others willingly. She sensed it without any real evidence to back it up, yet he wanted to share his grief and sorrow with her.

Why? She was flighty Mimi Van Hoyt, jumping from scandal to scandal and crisis to crisis. What would he possibly think she could offer that might help him?

But he was trusting her with this. She was important enough to him that he wanted her to know the things that were troubling him.

The weight of that trust burned inside her. She mattered to him and she couldn't bear the idea of letting him down.

"I haven't been sleeping well since the ambush. Things have been…rough." He gave her a long look she couldn't quite interpret. "Until you came along."

"What do you mean?"

"I don't know why. There's no logical explanation. But since you've been here, everything seems…easier."

She stared at him, heat fluttering through her. How was she supposed to respond to that? She didn't have the first idea what to say. Acting purely on instinct, she crossed the room to where he stood by the window, looking out at the black winter night. She took Simone from his arms and set the dog on the carpet, where she sniffed her disapproval but trotted to the rug by the fire as Mimi took her place, wrapping her arms around him.

After a surprised moment, Brant yanked her against him and wrapped her tightly in his arms, burying his face in her neck.

"I'm so, so sorry, Brant. For you, for those men, for their families left behind. But take it from someone who has spent her life screwing up in one form or another, you did nothing wrong here. I don't know anything about it. But I know you and I'm certain you were doing your job to the best of your ability. I am also certain not one of those men who died would have acted differently if they had been the one making the decision."

He held on for a long time and she could feel his ragged breathing against her skin.

She didn't know how long they stood that way in a silence broken only by Simone's snuffly breathing and the fire's low crackling.

That tenderness she had first recognized earlier pulsed through her and she pressed her cheek against his chest, listening to his heartbeat while his warm breath stirred her hair.

She thought it the most natural thing in the world some time later when his mouth found hers, as inevitable as the tide and the moonrise and the spring thaw.

Chapter Ten

His mouth was firm and strong on hers and she leaned into him, relishing the solid heat of him. He tasted of cinnamon and mocha and Brant, and she couldn't get enough.

The world outside the walls of this modest ranch-house could be a scary place, full of pain and war and betrayals, but right now none of that mattered. In Brant's arms, she was safe.

His hand caressed her cheek with a sweetness and gentleness that nearly had her bursting into tears. In all her twenty-six years, not a single, solitary soul had ever looked at her like Brant was gazing at her, as if she meant the world to him

"You're so lovely," he murmured. "More beautiful than any picture in any magazine. I sometimes look at you and can't believe you're real."

He cared about her. She saw the tenderness in his eyes, sensed it in his kiss. He wasn't simply trying to claim bragging rights that he'd been with Mimi Van Hoyt, as so many other men had tried, for some kind of a notch in his holster or whatever weapon an officer in the Army Rangers would carry.

Brant had feelings for her. A soft, seductive warmth bloomed inside of her, like the ice plants along the shore unfurling at the first morning rays of the sun, and she wanted to stay here all night and bask in it.

"I'm very real," she murmured. It seemed vitally important that he understand. "Everything else, the magazine covers and everything, that's the illusion."

She wrapped her arms around his neck and pulled his mouth to hers. This was real too, his kiss and the emotions swirling around them, the tenderness that engulfed them.

She was vaguely aware of him moving back to the sofa and pulling her across his lap, of his hands warm and sure under her sweater, of the rasp of his evening stubble on her skin, the solid strength of him against her.

They kissed for a long time, until they were both breathing hard and she burned brighter than the flames in the woodstove.

"We have to stop," he finally said, his voice ragged.

"Why?"

He pressed his forehead to hers. "Two days ago you nearly lost a baby. As much as I want you right now, I don't think the timing is the greatest."

"Dr. Dalton gave me the green light to resume normal activities," she reminded him, trying to keep the pleading note from her voice.

His mouth quirked into that sexy smile she adored.

"I think we both know that when this happens between us—and it *will* happen between us—it's going to be anything but normal."

Heat scorched her cheeks, even as his words sparked an answering tug of desire.

"You need to rest if you're going to take care of that baby."

His big, square-tipped fingers covered her abdomen and she felt the heat of him through the knit of her sweater as he touched her gently.

Just like that, the blasted pregnancy hormones kicked in and those ever-lurking tears pricked behind her eyelids.

Oh, how she wished she had chosen someone like Brant to be her baby's father. Someone good and strong and honorable. Not someone *like* him, she amended. There was no one like him. She wished she had waited for Brant himself, the kind of man who would treasure her and their child, who would be eager to step up and take responsibility for the life they had created together.

Marco's harsh words echoed in her ears. *"Your problem...take care of it...I won't let you ruin my life because you're too stupid to take a damn pill."*

He acted as if their brief affair had been entirely Mimi's fault, as if she had tied him to the bed and seduced him.

"Let me know when you've taken care of it," he had ordered. "I'm marrying Jess, Mimi. You know that. This little *oops* of yours changes nothing. What we had was thrilling and exciting, sure. You're Mimi Van Hoyt. But we both knew it was only temporary and that I always had Jessalyn waiting."

He wanted her to take care of it and she would, just

not the way Marco intended. Mimi would raise her child and love her and never, *ever* make her feel overlooked or unwanted.

And she would always regret that she hadn't waited for a man like Brant, someone who would cherish their child, who would toss her into the air and read bedtime stories and teach her how to ride a bicycle.

But as usual, she had screwed everything up.

"What's wrong?" he murmured.

She couldn't tell him, of course. He would think she was ridiculous, or worse, that she wanted him to rush in and rescue her from her mistakes.

"Just tired, that's all. I feel like I'm always tired."

He kissed her forehead and stood up from the sofa with her still in his arms, a feat of sheer muscle she doubted any other man of her acquaintance could manage.

"You should be sleeping. Come on, then. Let's get you to bed."

She didn't want to leave the shelter of his arms, where she could pretend even for a little while that this was anything but a deliciously sweet dream.

She wrapped her arms around his neck as he carried her down the hall to her bedroom. He set her on the bed, then kissed her again with breathtaking gentleness. "You and I need to have a long talk in the morning, when we've both got clearer heads."

"About what?"

"I've got five months left in Afghanistan. I hope I'm back before the baby's born and then it's looking like there's a chance I'll be stationed at Los Alamitos on a special assignment for a while. That's not so far from L.A. We can figure this out, Mimi. We will."

Unease clutched at her heart but she ignored it and

forced herself to smile. Couldn't she let herself be carried along in the dream for a little while longer?

"Good night."

He gave her that rare smile she found so unbearably appealing then closed the door quietly behind him.

Mimi sat on the bed long after he'd left, her emotions a wild tangle and a hundred thoughts chasing themselves around her head.

One of those emotions clamored to the fore, drowning out all the others.

She was in love with Brant.

Completely. Irreversibly.

Of all her ridiculous stunts, the scandals and the gossip and the poor decision-making, falling for an honorable, decent man had to be right near the top.

How could she have been so foolish? She was in the worst possible place in her life to fall in love. She was pregnant and alone and scared, on the brink of the biggest publicity nightmare her father could ever imagine.

The father of her baby was marrying someone else first thing tomorrow morning, for heaven's sake.

And yet in typical Mimi style, somehow she had complicated everything by falling head over heels in love with a solemn special forces officer who had a deep core of honor running through him.

Worse even than her own insanity was the terrifying fact that this decent, honorable man was cracked enough to think he might actually want some kind of future with *her.*

How insane was that? The tabloid princess and the war hero. The paparazzi would be euphoric.

She flopped back onto the bed, palms pressed over her eyes as nausea slicked through her.

The moment her pregnancy started to manifest itself, the entire celebrity press corps would be orgasmic trying to figure out who the father was. If she and Marco had succeeded in squelching any rumors about their liaison—and she had to believe they had, since not even a whisper had come out—attention would then shift to whomever she showed up with next.

Maybe she could hide out here at Western Sky for the next six months and then just tell people she had pulled a Madonna and secretly gone to some third world country to adopt a baby.

Nobody would buy it. Every corner of her life would be scrutinized.

She couldn't allow Brant to be dragged into the ugliness of her world, into that morass of endless cameras and shouting questions and rampant speculation about every minute detail of her personal life.

She'd been in the spotlight since she turned sixteen, when some intrepid photographer with a long lens had first snapped a picture of her sunbathing topless on her father's yacht in the Mediterranean.

She despised the constant attention, though she had to admit she had utilized it on occasion to tweak her father about something or other. She'd been in car chases with the paparazzi, she'd found them digging through her garbage and peeking in her windows.

How could she drag Brant into that world? She would destroy him, would take all that was good and right about him and ensnarl him in the sordid circus of her world.

She couldn't do that to him.

She loved him too much.

Those damn tears burned behind her eyes again and this time she couldn't stop one from trickling down.

She would have to leave. What other choice did she have? If she didn't break things off with him in a way that left no doubt in his mind that she didn't want to further their relationship, she had a powerful suspicion he would stubbornly continue trying to rush to her rescue. That was the sort of man he was.

But if she extricated herself from his world now, he would soon forget about this little interlude in his life. He would return to his career, to his life, to his dedication in the soldiers who served under him.

No one would ever connect him to Mimi Van Hoyt and her baby with the mysterious paternity.

She hated the very idea of it. But wouldn't it be far better to make a clean break now rather than later, after she had sucked him into her world, exposed him to the paparazzi, tarnished all that goodness?

Something bright and hopeful in her heart seemed to shrivel as she picked up her cell phone.

She turned it on, the first time she had bothered since she arrived at the ranch and she found more than a dozen texts and voicemail messages waiting for her.

Probably the vast majority of them were from Verena, her personal assistant. She was too cynical to hope any of them might be from her father. She could drop off the grid for months and the most intense emotion Werner would allow himself wouldn't be worry for his oldest child's safety but probably relief that Mimi was keeping her wild escapades out of the public eye for a while.

She didn't listen to any of the messages before she went to her favorites list and hit Verena's cell phone number, right at the top, where Verena had programmed it for her since Mimi was apparently too stupid to do even that.

Her assistant answered before Mimi even heard a ring on the other end.

"Where are you?" Verena Dumond sounded as ruffled as Mimi had ever heard the hyperefficient woman. "I've been trying to reach you for days. You were supposed to call me when you reached Ms. Bianca's so that I knew you arrived safely. When I didn't hear from you, I tried calling both your number and Ms. Bianca's but have had no luck."

"It's a long story," Mimi said, a vast understatement if she had ever uttered one. Her life felt fundamentally changed from the person she had been the last time she saw Verena and she was exhausted suddenly just thinking about all that had happened.

"Listen, I've had a change of plans," she said. "I know I intended to stay for another few days but I've changed my mind. I need you to make travel arrangements for me to leave as soon as possible."

"Will you be returning to Malibu?"

Mimi mentally scanned her options. She absolutely didn't want to return to California until long after Marco and Jessalyn enjoyed their oh-so-romantic wedding. She couldn't go to New York, where her father spent most of his time.

She gazed out the window and saw that the snow was falling again, fluttery soft flakes that didn't look as if they would amount to much before morning.

"Some place warm," she decided. "Is the St. Thomas house available?"

"I'll find out."

"Do you know what, Verena? I don't really care where I go. Just somewhere without snow. And I want to take the Lear this time, if it can be arranged."

She had flown commercial on her way out to Gwen's because none of the private planes had been available and she hadn't wanted to wait. Beyond that, she'd had some silly idea about not letting her father know where she could be found—as if he wouldn't have wormed the information out of Verena if he'd genuinely cared to know.

"I'll see what I can do but it might take me a few hours to route the plane to Idaho," her assistant said.

"In the morning should be fine. Oh, and I'll need a car service. The rental vehicle you arranged had a bit of a mishap."

"Again?" There was only the slightest note of condemnation in Verena's well-trained voice but Mimi bristled. Okay, she was a little tough on rental vehicles. That's why one rented, wasn't it?

"This time I couldn't help it. I was caught in a blizzard and slid off the road into a ditch."

"Good gracious."

"I'm all right."

That wasn't necessarily the truth. Mimi had a feeling she wouldn't be all right for a long time. When she left this place, this man, she would leave behind a huge jagged section of her heart.

"You're still at Gwen's?"

"Um, not exactly. I'm at the ranch but Gwen had a gallery showing in Europe and she's not here. After my accident, her landlord was kind enough to let me stay at the main house. But the address is the same. The Western Sky in Cold Creek Canyon."

Verena was silent for a long moment. "I see," she finally said in a carefully bland voice that didn't fool Mimi for a second.

"It's not what you think," Mimi protested.

"I don't think anything. I'm not paid for that." Verena used her frostiest voice and Mimi frowned.

"V., cut it out. Major Western was kind enough to rescue me from a creek when the SUV slid off the road. He's been…really wonderful."

"Will we be compensating him for his trouble, then?"

She let out a breath. Brant would hate that. He was proud enough that perhaps offering him money in return for helping her just might be enough to turn that soft affection in his eyes into disgust.

"I haven't decided how I'll repay him yet."

"I'm sure you'll figure out a way."

Again, that slight, barely perceptible note of condemnation in Verena's voice scraped her nerves. What really sucked was that Mimi knew she deserved it. Verena reported directly to her father, who paid her salary, so Mimi had done her best over the years to exaggerate her misdeeds to the other woman. If she went on a date with a man, she turned her version of the evening into a three-day orgy.

At this point in her life, Mimi doubted anyone would believe she had only ever been with three men, including her first love when she was eighteen—a rookie pro basketball player who had been sweet and nervous, even after they had dated for several weeks, her one-time fiancé who turned out to be gay, and Marco.

No sense trying to undo an image she'd spent years creating. Not in one phone call, anyway. "I'd like to make an early start in the morning. No later than eight a.m."

"I believe I can make those arrangements."

"I have no doubt." Mimi paused, thinking of her

years of resentment for Verena. Her handler, she'd always thought. Verena approved expenses, coordinated her schedule, worked with the rest of the staff at Mimi's Malibu and Bel Air houses, all while reporting every detail to Werner.

She might also have been a friend, if she hadn't been caught in the crossfire of the war between Mimi and her father.

"Verena, um, thank you. I…don't know what I would do without you."

After a long pause, Verena spoke, sounding uncharacteristically disconcerted. "You're welcome."

Mimi cut the connection and sat on the edge of the bed for a moment, her thoughts tangled.

If Verena, who knew Mimi probably better than anyone for the past five years, had such little respect and regard for her, how could she ever think she would be the sort of woman a man like Brant deserved?

She was right to leave, even if some small part of her was afraid she was making the biggest mistake of a life that had been chock full of them.

Chapter Eleven

What ever happened to that pregnancy glow she was supposed to be enjoying right about now?

Early the next morning, Mimi frowned at her reflection in the round guest bathroom mirror of the Western Sky. Her eyes were puffy, her skin red and blotchy.

No big deal. She had concealer and foundation and a half-dozen pair of designer sunglasses she could wear to hide away from the world.

She hadn't slept more than a few hours in the night. Mostly she had lay curled up on the bed, cuddling Simone close to her and watching the moon shift past the window.

She had never wished she could be Maura Howard more than she did right now. Oh, how she wanted to be just an ordinary woman who went grocery shopping and bought her clothes at a chain store and filled her car with gas every payday.

Maura Howard was a school teacher or a nurse or a librarian. Someone kind and uncomplicated, with simple tastes and ordinary parents.

Brant deserved someone like that, without baggage like Mimi's, someone he wouldn't be ashamed to introduce around Pine Gulch, someone who would fit in with the other Four Winds as they sat around the kitchen table sharing memories and swapping stories.

But she wasn't Maura and she could never be. She supposed the real challenge ahead of her was to somehow learn how to be happy being Mimi, but right now she didn't know how that could happen.

She finished her makeup and pulled her hair back into a loose twist at the nape of her neck, then quietly packed the rest of her belongings.

Simone planted her little haunches by the suitcases and whined, giving Mimi a mournful sort of look.

"We have to go, baby," she whispered. "Staying longer will only make everything so much harder."

Simone yipped sharply as if she wanted to disagree and Mimi shot a quick, nervous glance toward the door, afraid Brant would knock any moment.

Her dearest wish right now was that they could slip away to avoid a confrontation with Brant. Yes, it was cowardly, but it would be far easier to just sneak out without having to provide explanations or excuses.

She held her breath as she heard steps outside her door and she prayed he wouldn't knock and see her suitcases piled by the door. To her vast relief, he walked away and a moment later she heard the outside door open and close.

No doubt he was heading out to take care of the horses. Judging by the past few days, she had a narrow window of less than an hour for the car service to come while he was otherwise occupied.

Verena had texted her that the car should be arriving close to eight, which was still ten minutes away, so Mimi let Simone out, keeping a careful eye on the barn while she waited and let the dog take care of her business.

As she stood on the backsteps to the ranchhouse, she soaked in one more view of the exquisite surroundings. She hoped so much that Brant would decide not to sell, despite the work she had put into sprucing up the place.

Whether he wanted to admit it or not, he needed the peace of this place. Even if he could only spend a few weeks here each year, this was his home. She had a powerful feeling that if he sold it, he would regret it for the rest of his life.

Simone finished up quickly and hurried back up the porch steps, as eager as Mimi to get out of the bitter cold.

She returned to the front room, keeping a nervous eye on the clock while she struggled to write some sort of note to Brant. Nothing seemed adequate so she simply wrote, "I had to go. We both know it's for the best. Thank you for everything. I'll never forget my time here."

She was just signing her name when she heard the approach of a vehicle and then the doorbell.

Oh, thank heavens. She propped the note on the kitchen table where he couldn't miss it and hurried to the front door, where her suitcases was already piled up.

"I have to put my dog in her crate but you can carry the rest of my luggage out—" Her words to what she thought was the car service driver died in her throat at the familiar strobe of cameras flashing, again and again and again.

Paparazzi, only a handful—maybe two still photographers and a couple of videographers. But here in the quiet of an Idaho winter's morning, it felt like a mass invasion.

Like an idiot, she couldn't think past her shock that they had found her, couldn't move as the questions started flying.

"Where you going, Mimi?"

"Is it true you had an ultrasound at a clinic in Pine Gulch? Are you pregnant, Mimi?"

"Who's the father, Mimi? Is it Prince Gregor?"

Panic flared through her, hot and bright. Jake and Maggie must have a leak in their office staff or one of their other patients must have seen her while she was there.

Whoever it was, someone had tipped off the rabid horde and thrown Mimi into the middle of a disaster.

Today was Marco's wedding. Couldn't they have waited one more day? Would some enterprising gossip columnist somehow make the connection she least wanted out?

Simone continued yipping. Mimi knew she needed to do something, say something, but she couldn't seem to make the connection work between her frenzied brain and the rest of her.

Just as she started to edge back into the house, a new unwelcome sound distracted her—the pounding of horse's hooves and harsh male voice rising above all the others.

"What the hell do you vultures think you're doing?"

Brant. She closed her eyes, fighting the urge to sit on the steps and burst into sobs. He rode up like some kind of damned avenging angel, big and hard and dangerous, plowing the horse right through the middle of the small group of photographers, who had to quickly move out of his way before he mowed them all down. Of course, they didn't stop filming for a second, she saw with resigned dismay.

Brant looked furious, more angry than she had ever seen him. And a livid Army Ranger was a dangerous force to behold.

At the porch steps, he slid down from the horse, threw the rains around the top railing of the porch and bounded up the steps to her side.

"Everything past that gate you went through off the main road is private property. Every damn one of you is trespassing."

"Go away," she hissed to him, barely able to breathe past her misery. "You're only going to make everything worse."

He stared at her, confusion on his features, then his gaze narrowed. "No," he answered, his jaw tight and his eyes a deep midnight-blue.

Before she could argue, he threw one powerful arm around her shoulders and yanked her against him, then turned back around to the gawking photographers.

He was a formidable man, with his powerful build and his steely Army commando stare, and though she wanted him anywhere else in the world than right here beside her, she couldn't help appreciating how the paparazzi almost as one took an instinctive step back.

"You have got exactly three minutes to get into your vehicles and slither back to whatever slime spit you out. I'm calling the sheriff, who just happens to be a good friend of mine. He'll have no problem rushing deputies up here to haul every one of your asses into jail for trespassing and harassment. I'm sure he won't mind confiscating all that nice camera equipment, either."

"Who's the cowboy, Mimi?" one intrepid still photographer, she thought was named Harvey, yelled at her.

"Is he the father of your baby?" another shouted.

"Does Werner know he's going to be a grandpa?" another added.

She was hyperventilating. She could feel the panic attack swell at the edges of her subconscious and she did her best to fight it back.

Brant took one look at her and yanked her back into the house, slamming the door behind them.

To her horror, he reached into the coat closet by the door and pulled out a lethal-looking shotgun.

The sight of it managed to shock her back to reality. She would have time to freak out when she was on the way to the airport but right now she had to keep it together, for damage control if nothing else.

She grabbed his arm. "What are you doing? Put that away!"

He flexed his muscle to keep the shotgun out of her reach and she felt as if she were touching one of those giant slabs of granite peeking through the snow near the river.

"I'm not going to use it. But they don't know that, do they?"

She had to stop him. If the man had no sense of self-preservation, she had to do what she could to protect him. "You have no idea what you're dealing with here. You are way out of your league, Major."

He raised an eyebrow. "I've spent five of the last seven years in heavy combat. I think I can take care of myself against a bunch of photographers with lip rings and ponytails."

"You can't!" she exclaimed but he completely ignored her and opened the front door and walked out onto the porch with the shotgun cradled in his arms.

Mimi let out a sob of frustration and covered her face with her hands.

"Two minutes," Brant barked and then he worked the pump action on the shotgun with that distinctive *ch-ch* sound no one could mistake for anything else.

The paparazzi had been milling around by their vehicles, probably wondering just how far he would go to kick them off or hoping they could squeeze in one last picture of her.

At the sight of Brant in warrior mode, aiming a firearm at them, they snapped a few more images and climbed into their vehicles.

Through the window, Mimi watched them head down the road in three SUVs, tires spitting snow and gravel behind them.

As soon as they were out of sight, Brant returned to the house looking as pleased as if he'd just fought back an entire contingent of enemy combatants single-handedly.

"They won't bother you again," he said with such confidence that she couldn't help herself, she curled up her fist and smacked his shoulder as hard as she could.

She hadn't had much force to put behind it but at least shock had been on her side. He stared at her. "What was that that for?"

"How could you be so stupid?"

"You don't really believe I called those bastards, do you?"

She raked a hand through her hair. "Of course not. You would never do that. Anyway, would you have chased them off with a shotgun if you'd been the one to call them in the first place?"

"How do you think they found you?"

She sat on the sofa and covered her face in her hands, wondering how she was going to explain all this to Verena, to her friends, to her father.

"Any number of ways. I'm guessing someone at the clinic saw me, despite Jake and Maggie's best efforts. Or perhaps someone on their staff wasn't as discreet as he should have been."

"I'll find out," he vowed, with enough menace in his voice that Mimi had to swallow a whimper.

"It doesn't really matter how they found me. The important thing is that they have."

She punched him again, furious all over again that he would step up to defend her, even if one tiny corner of her heart glowed at the gesture.

"You have no idea what a mess you just thrust yourself into. A shotgun, for heaven's sake. What were you thinking? You look like you just stepped off a damn wanted poster. They're going to be calling you Mimi's Outlaw or something absurd like that."

"You think I care about that?"

"Maybe not now, right this moment, in the heat of battle, as it were. But what about a few days from now when you can't walk outside without a dozen clicking cameras? Or when you return to duty and all your men start calling you Mimi's Outlaw, too?"

"You think I care about that? It worked, didn't it? They're gone."

She curled her hands into fists. "I don't believe this! Can you really be so completely naive?"

He aimed a measure of that menacing look at her.

"Naive? I've been leading troops into combat for almost a decade. Naivete is in short supply on the battlefield."

"What else would you call it? You solved nothing with your little shotgun act. Who do you think is going to be camped out at the end of your driveway on public property until your leave ends?"

"So what?"

She picked up the still-yipping Simone and set her into her cage. "So they're cockroaches. You might stomp on a few and scare off a few more but they're only going to go call their friends. Before you know it, you turn on the lights of your kitchen at night and they'll be everywhere."

How could she have done this to him? Dragged him into the ugliness of her world?

She had to end this, now.

"Brant, you had no right to come charging in like that to my rescue. I didn't ask for your help and I didn't need it."

"My house, my decision." He glared right back at her.

Mimi let out a long breath, despising herself for what she knew she had to do.

She had no choice. The rumors were already flying about her pregnancy. *Is he the father?* one of the paparazzi had yelled. Everyone would be speculating about it and she couldn't allow Brant's name to be dragged through the mud and muck of her world, anymore than it already would be from those pictures.

She curled her hands into fists, digging her nails into her skin. "You had no right," she said again. "Now everybody will know I've been staying here with you.

There's no way I can keep it a secret after you pulled such a ridiculous stunt."

As she had half-hoped, half-dreaded, she saw some of his anger at the photographers shift toward her. "I didn't realize keeping your presence here a secret was our priority," he said stiffly.

Of all the silly, foolhardy things she had done, all the mistakes and the scandals, she had never regretted anything as much as what she was about to do.

And she had never despised herself more.

"Of course I wanted it to stay a secret. Do you really think I want these few days to become public?"

"I don't know. You tell me."

She forced herself to give him her famous ditzy smile and spoke in a lighthearted tone, though the words cut her throat like razor blades. "Of course not. I'm Mimi Van Hoyt. As sweet as you've been, Brant, you're... well, not exactly my type."

A muscle flexed in his jaw but other than that, he went completely still. "Your type?"

"You know. Men like Prince Gregor or an A-list actor or one of the Kennedys. That's what I'm used to."

"Yes, I can certainly see why I would present a change of pace."

He was furious now. She could see the embers flaring to life in his eyes.

"I'm only thinking of you, Brant." That, at least, was the truth, but she twisted her tone to make it sound as if it meant the opposite. "You don't want your name linked with mine, either. You have your career to consider. What would your commanding officers think if they found out you spent your leave cavorting with someone like me?"

He crossed his arms over his chest. "Was there cavorting? Somehow I must have missed the cavorting."

She shrugged. "Just like you're completely missing the point. Our lives exist on different planes, Brant. Surely you can see that. What do we possibly have in common?"

"I thought we were coming to care about each other."

His careful words and the intensity behind them stabbed at her and she forced herself not to sway.

"Sure, I kissed you a few times because you were here and, let's face it, you're hot in that cowboy/soldier, macho kind of way. I'm really sorry if you might have gotten the wrong idea and thought those kisses meant more than they did."

She saw hurt and disbelief in his eyes and she had to dig her nails tighter into her palms to keep from reaching for him.

She put on her fake Mimi smile again. "Look, I'm not sure things are finished with my baby's father, despite what I told you before. You've really helped me put things into perspective there."

The second part also wasn't a lie but Mimi had always been good at twisting the truth to suit her purposes. And right now her purpose was to end things with Brant, once and for all, despite the devastation to her heart.

"Until I know for sure it's really over, I just can't complicate everything by becoming entangled with someone else. Especially not someone so…unsuitable."

She heard the sound of a vehicle pulling up out front. Either one of the photographers had a death wish or her car service had just arrived. Since Brant still wasn't looking quite convinced, Mimi decided she had no choice but to play her trump card.

She gave him her hard, polished smile and picked up

the note she had begun to write for him. She smoothly pocketed that one—even as terse as it had been, it somehow seemed far too personal. Instead, she picked another piece of paper from the stack and scribbled a phone number on it.

"Look, here's my assistant's cell number. Her name is Verena Dumond and she's a pain in the you-know-what but she's frighteningly efficient. Just let her know how much you think your time and effort is worth for the few days I spent here and she can cut you a check for any expenses I incurred while I was here. Gas, food, whatever. And don't worry, I'll make sure to tell her to throw in a nice bonus for all your trouble."

Brant stared at the slip of paper in her slim hand that jangled with silvery bracelets.

Ah.

Here she was at last—the Mimi frigging Van Hoyt he had expected to encounter when he dragged her out of her SUV in the middle of a blizzard.

She was condescending and abrasive and right now he was pretty sure he despised her.

He didn't know what was truth and what was an act. Though her words sounded convincing enough—snobbish and bitchy though they were—there was something in her eyes, some shadow, that didn't mesh with what she was saying.

He was so busy trying to sort it all out that he almost missed the sound of another vehicle approaching the house.

When he caught it, he picked up the shotgun again and walked out onto the porch, just as a man dressed in a black uniform stepped out of an SUV with tinted windows.

The driver froze when he saw a man on the front porch holding a Remington but Brant had to give the guy credit for not crawling back into the limo and speeding down the driveway.

"I'm here to pick up a Ms. Howard. Do I have the wrong address?"

"No," Mimi answered briskly from behind him before Brant could get any words out. "I'm here. I've got a few more bags inside if you could be so kind."

"Not at all, Miss."

Brant caught the chauffer's quick double-take when he recognized Mimi but he concealed it quickly, too well-trained to react more than that first flash of surprise.

"You're leaving," Brant said, flatly stating the obvious. If he hadn't been so angry, he might have perhaps noticed her luggage by the door.

"Yes. There's a plane waiting for me right now at the Jackson Hole airport."

"Were you going to say anything to me or just disappear without a word?"

Something flickered in her eyes for just a moment then she gave him that bright, fake smile again. "I was starting to write a thank you note when the photographers showed up."

"A note. You planned to leave me a note."

"Well, yes. Along with Verena's phone number, of course."

He had never been so furious. The rage swept over him like an August firestorm and he had to draw in several deep breaths to beat it back.

"You're angry with me." She actually had the gall to sound surprised.

"That's one word for it," he bit out.

"I'm sorry for that. But since Dr. Dalton told me it's safe to travel now, I decided there was no logical reason to delay the inevitable."

"None at all."

Underneath the anger, lurking several layers down like a hidden reservoir under the desert, was a vast, endless pool of pain, aimed mostly at himself.

How could he have been such an idiot? He had actually spent the night dreaming about building a future with her. Raising her child somewhere away from the cameras and the craziness.

The lunacy of it just about took his breath away. How could he ever have thought Mimi might want that with someone like him?

As sweet as you've been, Brant, you're...well, not exactly my type.

The chauffeur returned just then and quickly picked up the rest of her luggage.

"Will there be anything else, Ms. Howard?"

Mimi handed him Simone's pink crate. For some crazy reason, the sight of that silly little dog gazing at him with big soulful eyes affected Brant more than he would have believed possible.

"That's everything," Mimi said. "Thank you. I'll be just a few moments more."

The man tapped the bill of his cap respectfully and then left the house. When he was gone, Mimi smiled at Brant but it wasn't the winsome smile he had come to adore these past few days.

"Well, thank you again for not turning me out that first night and for helping me through the last few days."

She used exactly the same tone she used with the chauffeur. Impersonal. Polite. Detached.

"So that's it."

"I suppose it is." She paused for a moment. "Be safe, won't you?"

Her voice caught, just a bit, on the words and he gave her a careful look to see if he could find a crack beneath her veneer but she was once more cool and remote.

"Don't forget to send your expenses to Verena. I'll tell her to be expecting your call."

She stepped forward, brushed her cool lips against his cheek, pulled down her sunglasses from atop her head and walked out of the house and out of his life.

Chapter Twelve

Brant didn't know when he had ever been so tired.

He'd managed to doze a little on the plane from the military hospital at the Ramstein Air Base in Germany, but except for that restive sleep, he had been awake for close to twenty-four hours. Right now, all he wanted was to crawl into his bed, pull the covers over his head and crash for the next twenty-four.

The pain from his arm and side growled at him and gnawed with sharp teeth. He had a bottle of pain pills in his duffel but he was doing his best not to rely on them. He had a feeling that after a full day of travel, he might not have much choice.

He was also painfully aware that his decision to drive from Idaho Falls might not have been the greatest idea he'd ever come up with. He hadn't been behind the wheel since the incident nearly three weeks earlier and he hadn't realized how difficult it was to drive one-handed, especially when he'd injured his dominant right side. He was learning more about ambidexterity than he ever cared to know.

But he had made it this far. Only a few more miles and he would be home. As his eyes scanned the road in Cold Creek Canyon, he was struck once again by the familiar rugged beauty of the place. He could think of nowhere more gorgeous than Cold Creek Canyon in July, with the mountains a deep, soothing green, the creek flashing silver in the sunset, the scattered patches of columbine and yarrow among the towering stands of pine and fir.

This was home and he had never been more grateful to be driving up this canyon road.

Something sweet and calming seemed to wash through him as he turned onto the Western Sky access road. He drove under the ranch's log arch with a little prayer of gratitude in his heart that he had reached the momentous decision not sell the place.

He didn't know what had changed during his time here with Mimi but after he returned to Afghanistan, he hadn't been able to shake the strange assurance that he couldn't sell the ranch. Not now. No matter where he traveled, the Western Sky would always be his home and he couldn't think about someone else living here.

Some day he might have a family of his own—though that time seemed a lifetime away. If he sold the Western Sky, his children would never know their heritage, never know they belonged to such a place of peace in the world.

Besides, if he had sold the ranch, where would he recover for the next month? The impersonal base housing in Georgia, where he had nothing to do but sit and watch television all day?

Oh, he probably could have stayed in a room at Winder Ranch with Easton. The house there had eight bedrooms, after all, and she was living all by herself. But Easton would have wanted to fuss over him and he would have been obliged to let her. This way was much better, here where he could be on his own with only his memories.

The heaviest runoff was done this late in the year, he noted as he drove up the access road to the ranchhouse. The creek burbled along beside the road with cheerful abandon. He was definitely going to spend some serious time with a fly rod while he was here if he could get his blasted arm to cooperate.

In front of the ranchhouse, any thoughts of fly fishing flew from his head. He braked the rental vehicle and climbed out, frowning as he looked around.

What on earth?

This was *not* the same place he had seen in February—even discounting the fact that everything wasn't buried in the two feet of snow he'd left behind when he returned to Afghanistan.

The barn and sprawling outbuildings sported a bright new coat of rustic red paint, the fences had been repaired, the sagging spot on the porch roof looked flush and level. Two white rocking chairs graced the long front porch, angled to take in the best view of the mountains and instead of the weedy, barren flowerbeds lining the front porch, a riot of color exploded.

He climbed out of the rental car and leaned a hip against the door, trying to absorb all these small changes that combined to make a huge difference.

The Western Sky looked charming and well kept, something he hadn't seen here in, well, ever.

Easton e-mailed him she had hired a new caretaker to replace Gwen but she hadn't said much about her, other than it was someone who had a background in renovation. At the time, he had been too busy planning a couple major raids and hadn't paid as much attention to her e-mail as he should have. He completely trusted Easton to do what was best for him and for the ranch and he'd told her so.

She had come through, in spades. Easton had never mentioned his new caretaker was a genius. His home looked clean and cheerful, the kind of place where a man could kick off his boots and all his worries.

Except for the memories.

Brant let out a breath, trying his best not to think about that last miserable scene with Mimi, when the paparazzi had stood just off the porch there, flashing their cameras and shouting their questions and sending his foolish dreams of a happily-ever-after with her drifting away into the bitter February air like the smoke from the chimney.

He should have known she would haunt him here. He had half-expected it, he just didn't know those memories would be waiting to ambush him the moment he drove onto the ranch.

She was everywhere here. Sitting on the sofa inside watching Hitchcock movies, playing poker at the kitchen table, painting the guest room with those adorable little paint freckles dotting her face.

He closed his eyes and once more saw her heading down those very steps as she walked out of his life.

That last scene had played vividly in his head for months. He had pored over the memory again and again, sifting through her words, her expression, her tone of voice.

What was truth and what was lie?

Once he had stopped reeling from the cold finality of their parting, he had begun to think maybe Mimi hadn't been exactly truthful with him in that last ugly scene. There had been something not quite right in the tone of her voice and the overbright smile.

Big surprise there, that she might have been less than honest with him, since she'd spent her entire time at the Western Sky weaving one lie or another. But he had reached the inevitable conclusion that she wanted him out of her life. That much had been abundantly clear.

Oh, he'd had to deal with some questions and some ribbing after those pictures of the two of them together had been printed. A few junior officers had tried to make tasteless, off-color jokes about it, but only once. Brant had cut them off with a steely glare and a few well-placed threats.

Then had come that brief, shocking statement a few weeks after he returned to Afghanistan where she announced to the world she was having a baby from in vitro fertilization and an unknown sperm donor. Even thousands of miles away in the middle of a war zone, he had seen a little of the controversy and doubt that announcement had sparked.

He had been watching for paparazzi coverage of her—pathetic on his part, he knew—but other than a few well-documented shopping trips for baby clothes and maternity things every so often, Mimi seemed to be keeping a low profile.

She would be due in only a few months. Not that he was counting or anything.

He wasn't going to think about her. Because of his injuries, he had nearly a month in Pine Gulch before he needed to report to his new assignment at Los Alamitos.

In that time, he planned to give his body a chance to heal while he rode horses and fished and savored the serenity here.

But first he needed to sleep for the next day or two.

He grabbed his duffel out of the backseat of the rental and started for the house, interested to see if the inside had received the same spruce-up. He had only taken one step up the porch stairs when he saw a big yellow Labrador retriever round the house with something pink and flowery in its mouth.

The dog barreled to a cartoonlike stop when he caught sight of Brant and then he dropped whatever was in his mouth and started barking—a deep, excited hey-we-have-company kind of bark.

Brant barely had seconds to react to that when another little animal rounded the corner of the house and he could do nothing but stare at the fluffy white furball with bright black eyes as it let out an ecstatic yip and headed right for him.

It couldn't be Mimi's silly little dog. He knew it couldn't be. But why would another bichon frise be wandering around the Western Sky?

The question was completely yanked out of his mind a second later when a figure—this time a human— followed the dogs.

She was pushing a wheelbarrow loaded with flowers and she was laughing, her green eyes bright in the long, stretched-out shadows of an early-July evening. "Hey, come back here with that, you rascal. You think I'm going to want to wear my gardening hat now that it's all slobbery and gross?"

He couldn't think straight and for moment he wondered if he was having some kind of pain-induced hallucination. He dropped his duffel and curled his good hand into a fist, not quite believing this was real.

Mimi must have seen the car then. He watched her do the same sort of double take as the yellow Lab and then she turned toward him.

She was hugely pregnant and ethereally lovely, with her curly dark hair swept up in a loose style on top of her head and her skin glowing with color and health.

Something tugged at his heart, something fierce and powerful. For one insane moment, he wanted nothing so much as to rush to her, sweep her into his arms and twirl her in the air again and again.

He saw the shock in her eyes, saw her features go a shade paler, and as he stood with one foot on the porch step, the whole wall of denial he had so carefully constructed tumbled down, brick by painful brick.

He was in love with her. Nothing had changed. All those months of trying to tell himself she meant nothing to him, that he could turn his back on what they might have had just as easily as she apparently could, were meaningless.

He let out a breath, furious with himself and with her. "What do you think you're doing here?" he bit out.

"You… You're not supposed to be home for another ten days."

"You're not supposed to be here at all," he snapped, wondering how she had known his travel schedule, the original one from before his injury. "What are you doing here, Mimi?"

She shrugged, still looking stunned and completely breathtaking. And nervous, he suddenly realized. She looked nervous to see him.

"Oh, you know. Just putting in some flowering

annuals to help fill in the holes in your beds. The perennials won't really come into their full color until next summer but it will be glorious by this time next year."

"What are you doing *here?* At my ranch?"

She moved closer, the guilty expression on her features fading to one of concern. "Are you all right? You look a little pale."

He would never admit to her or anyone else that his knees were beginning to go weak at the pain screeching from his injuries. "Mimi! Answer me. What are you doing at Western Sky, planting annuals in my flower beds?"

She gnawed her lip. "Um, I live here. At least for another couple of days. I guess I'll be moving quicker than I'd planned. We really didn't think you were coming home until the week after next. What happened? Why did your plans change?"

He didn't want to explain to her that he'd spent the past two weeks in the burn unit at Ramstein. He hadn't told anyone, not even Easton, and it certainly wasn't Mimi's business that he had been injured while trying to yank two Marines from a burning Humvee hit by an IED while traveling directly in front of his vehicle in a convoy.

Nor did he want to explain that he was becoming light-headed from the pain and needed to sit down before he fell over. Wouldn't that be a kick in the butt?

"Plans change," he said.

"Well, it would have been nice to know your arrangements," she said with a slightly disgruntled tone. "I planned to move out of Gwen's cabin before you arrived. Easton and I both thought it would probably be best."

"Easton knows you're here." She would have had to

know, yet she hadn't said a word to him in their frequent e-mail correspondence, the little sneak.

"Yes," she said warily.

The truth hit him in a rush, then. Everything seemed to shift into focus—the flower beds, the fresh paint on the barn, the hundreds of little changes around the ranch.

"You're the caretaker she's been raving about. The one who has poured so much effort into the house."

Guilt again flitted across her features. "Yes."

None of this made sense. He didn't know what to think. "Why do I always feel like I've stepped into some alternate universe when you're around?"

"I'm sorry."

"No, you're not. You like leaving people off balance, making sure they have no idea what to expect next. It's part of the whole Mimi charm."

She looked as if she wanted to disagree but she only moved toward the porch. "I'm sorry," she said again. "But if you don't mind, I really need to sit down. My feet are a little swollen right now."

Since that matched exactly with his own hidden agenda that he'd rather be tortured than admit, he shrugged and headed up the stairs, dropping his duffel by the door.

"Before I sit down, I'm going to get a drink of water," she said. "I'm parched. Can I grab you one?"

He shrugged, not eager to accept anything from her even though the thought of the pure mountain spring water that came from the tap here was undeniably enticing.

He waited until she went into the house before he sagged into one of the rocking chairs and let out the tight breath that had been holding in all the pain from his injuries.

Simone had apparently missed him, if no one else had. The minute he sat down, she jumped onto his lap with an eager yip and he carefully kept her away from the bandages wrapped around his abdomen.

The Lab, not to be outdone, curled up at his boots, perfectly at home there.

Brant didn't care, he was just grateful to have a moment to absorb the shock of finding Mimi here in real life when he thought he would only be encountering the ghost of her memory.

She bustled out of the house a moment later with a small tray with two tall glasses, a sliced apple and some crackers and cheese. Seeing her so at home in his house gave him an odd feeling, a tangled mix of consternation and contentment.

While he drank, she lowered herself carefully into the rocker next to him and he watched over the top of his glass, fascinated with the cumbersome process. She looked round and lush and beautiful.

Once she sat, she sipped her own water, then set it on the arm of the rocker.

As the silence dragged on, it occurred to Brant that she was watching him as warily as if he were an IED being disarmed by an explosives ordnance disposal team.

He wanted to ask how she had been feeling. How was the baby? Did she know if she was having a boy or a girl and had she picked out names? Was she nervous about becoming a mother?

All those questions rattled through him but he forced himself to focus on the only thing that really mattered.

"Why are you here, Mimi?"

She chewed the corner of her lip again, and he remembered how delicious that mouth had tasted, how perfectly she had fit into his arms, how for one magical night he had allowed himself the most ridiculous dreams.

She finally sighed. "I convinced Easton to hire me. It's not her fault, honestly. Please don't blame her. I can be…persuasive when I set my mind to it."

"Why would you try to be persuasive?"

"I needed a place to stay away from all the craziness and…I like it here. It's peaceful and quiet and the people are so warm and kind to me. Easton and Maggie Dalton threw a baby shower for me last week. Isn't that great? And nearly everyone they invited showed up. I got the most darling clothes and toys you can imagine for the baby and you should see the crib quilt that Emery Cavazos made. It's a work of art that should be in a museum! You wouldn't believe how kind everyone here is to me."

She seemed so shocked and delighted that he didn't have the heart to tell her most of the people in Pine Gulch were kind to just about everyone.

"How long have you been here?"

"Since March, when Gwen moved to her house in Jackson Hole."

He couldn't seem to absorb it, even with the reality of her sitting beside him. How could she have spent five months in virtual seclusion out here, away from the crowds and the stores and the cameras?

"Why didn't the paparazzi mob you here? I haven't seen anything about you living on a ranch in eastern Idaho."

Not that he'd been looking, he assured himself.

"I made sort of a devil's bargain with them. I would show up once a month in California for a long weekend and go to a few parties, do a little shopping, strictly for their benefit, and in return they would leave me alone the rest of the time. Since my life here is pretty tame, there's not much to photograph except the occasional trip to the hardware store for paint and to the Gulch for lunch with Easton and Maggie and the rest of the friends I've made here."

He tried to picture her walking the crowded aisles of the hardware store and ordering greasy food at the café in town and pushing a cart around the grocery store and couldn't seem to make his imagination stretch that far.

"Why did no one in town happen to mention to me in those five months that Mimi Van Hoyt was living in my house?"

"Not in your house, technically. In Gwen's cabin."

He glared at her nitpicky correction and she sighed. "Easton knew you wouldn't like it so she purposely didn't say anything. Everyone else probably figured you already knew."

"You could have found a quiet place anywhere else on earth to hide out until you have the baby. There are other peaceful spots around the globe. Why did it have to be here."

"I like it here," she said again. "I really can't give you any other explanation than that. When Gwen told me Easton was looking to hire someone to replace her as caretaker and continue the work I started fixing up the place, I called her right away and applied for the job."

He apparently had to have a long talk with Easton about hiding things from him and about keeping her busybody nose out of his affairs. But then Easton couldn't have known the whole story about what had happened between him and Mimi. He supposed he couldn't be too angry at her for allowing the one woman he least wanted to see to take over his ranch.

"I'm sorry it upsets you," Mimi went on carefully. "I honestly planned to finish everything up and be out of here before you returned."

"So you'll be moving out."

"Yes." She hesitated. "But I should probably tell you, in the interest of full disclosure, that I want Dr. Dalton to deliver my baby, so I'll be sticking around Pine Gulch until after the birth. Nate and Emery have offered me the use of one of the guest cabins at Hope Springs. Caroline and Wade Dalton also have been pushing me to stay at their guesthouse at the Cold Creek. I guess I have to choose now, don't I?"

Some petty part of him wanted to tell her she had to choose right now, tonight. But she was hugely pregnant and he couldn't just toss her out into the cold, as much as he would like to. "No rush," he lied. "Take a few days to make up your mind where you want to go."

The way he felt right now, he figured he wouldn't be crawling out of bed for the next day and a half so he likely wouldn't even run into her again.

Before he could rein it in, his wayward imagination flashed a picture of falling asleep with Mimi next to him in his big bed, all her warmth and softness curled against him, with her dark curls drifting across his skin, with his hands splayed across that fascinating round belly....

He caught the direction of his gaze and frowned, disgusted at himself. Amazing what kind of crazy images could play with a man's head when he was exhausted and sore.

"I appreciate that," she said, and it took him a minute

to realize she was referring to his comment that she didn't have to leave immediately.

He wanted to tell her that was still his preference—that she go and take her little dog with her—but he decided to save his energy.

"Are you all right?" she asked after a long moment.

He blinked at her. "Why?"

"You seem…distracted."

Well, he couldn't take a deep breath because of the burns and he'd just endured three weeks of misery in a military hospital and he was pretty close to falling over from exhaustion.

Other than that, he was swell.

"Just surprised," he said, his voice coming out gruff. "I didn't expect to find you here—or anywhere, really, ever again. It's been a shock and I'm still reeling a little."

"Are you angry?"

Angry? That seemed a mild word when he thought of the heaviness in his heart these past four months.

No. *Angry* would imply he cared about her, that he had been hurt by what had happened between them.

"I would have to care to be angry," he answered. "Now if you'll excuse me, I've been traveling for a day and need to find my bed."

"Okay." She smiled but it wasn't the incandescent Mimi smile he remembered. This one was smaller and a little sad. "Welcome home, Major."

He inclined his head to answer her and pushed Simone onto the ground, then gripped the arms of the rocker and marshalled all his strength to rise.

He probably would have been fine and managed to go inside without her being any the wiser, but he misjudged the width of the rocking chair and his injured side brushed the wooden arm as he rose.

Pain clawed at him—fierce, unrelenting—and he couldn't contain one sharp inhale. His knees went weak and he had to sit back down, more carefully this time.

Mimi paled and was at his side in an instant. "What is it? What's wrong?"

"Nothing. I'm fine. Goodbye."

"You're not fine! You've been hurt, haven't you? That's why you're home early. That's why you're so pale and you're sweating, even here on the cool porch."

He didn't want her to know. She would probably rush right over to Winder Ranch and tell Easton, who was apparently her chatty new best friend.

"It's nothing," he repeated.

"Who's the liar now?" she snapped. "What happened? You might as well tell me. I can find out with few simple phone calls."

She was right. With her father's clout, she could probably worm out any detail of his life she ever wanted to know.

Anyway, the truth was easier. He was pretty sure he didn't have the energy to stand here and make up some elaborate story.

"No big deal. I suffered a little injury in an incident a few weeks ago."

Her face seemed to leach of what little color she had left. "How little? What kind of incident? Were you shot?"

He thought of the three weeks he'd spent in the burn unit of Ramstein and the surgeries and the skin grafts and the risks of infection he still faced. He almost thought he would have preferred a nice clean gunshot wound.

"No," he said shortly, hoping she would leave it at that. But of course, being Mimi, she didn't.

"What is it? Tell me, Brant." She spoke in a low, urgent voice, her eyes huge in her lovely face.

He was weak to let her affect him so much, but somehow her concern warmed a cold, achy corner of his heart.

"Burned. We were in a convoy traveling behind a Humvee that hit an IED. My arm and side sustained a little heat damage during the rescue effort." A nice way of saying second- and third-degree burns over a good portion of skin.

Chapter Thirteen

Mimi closed her eyes, trying not to picture the scene in her mind, the screams and the flames and the smell of burning flesh. She could clearly envision Brant rushing to the rescue, taking charge of the scene with that sense of command that was so innate.

She fought down tears, wondering why she seemed to spend so much time blubbering around him.

"You need to rest. I'm sorry I've kept you talking out here when you should be sleeping."

He didn't look as if he had the energy even to argue with her, though she still saw a shadow of the anger she fully deserved in his gaze.

"I'll start making arrangements to find another place to stay," she said. She hated the idea of leaving the Western Sky, but she owed him that, at least.

"Fine," he said shortly, and she caught the message

loud and clear. He wanted her gone. Beyond that, he didn't care what she did.

"Do you need any help with anything?"

His short laugh sounded icy cold. "From you? No thank you."

He rose abruptly, picked up his duffel from the porch and stalked into the house.

She deserved that. Mimi curled her fingers, doing her best to ignore the ache in her chest. He had every reason to detest her after the things she said to him. What else could she expect?

He was injured. She pictured again that shock of pain in his eyes when he had brushed against the chair. Foolish man. He was hurt and he hadn't even told his foster sister. Easton would have told Mimi if she'd known.

How could she leave him alone here at the ranch when he was in pain and possibly needing help?

Brant didn't want her here. She had made sure he wouldn't by pretending condescension and disdain. She couldn't complain now when her efforts paid off.

In her mind, those few days she had spent here with him possessed a magical, dreamlike quality, and she had wondered if she might have imagined the intensity of her feelings for him. Seeing him again answered that question. She was still in love with him, perhaps more now than she'd ever been. She had had five months to think about his strength and his honor, to vividly remember the safety and peace she found in his arms.

Because she loved him, she would leave this place she also loved. He deserved to have his home to himself, especially since he was injured and in pain.

She pressed a hand on her abdomen, to the little life growing there. "We'll be okay, kiddo," she whispered, repeating the mantra that had sustained her for five months.

She had used the same mantra during those first heartbreaking days after she left the ranch, when she told her father the news of her pregnancy, when she and her extensive team of lawyers met with Marco to convince him to formally relinquish any claim of paternity for the child and never speak of it again, which he had been only too eager to do. As far as Mimi was concerned, while the public statement that she had conceived via in vitro wasn't technically true, Marco had only been her baby's sperm donor, nothing more.

Seeing Brant again made her wish once more with all her heart that she had picked someone like him to father her child. But she wouldn't regret the course her life had taken.

She had grown more these past five months than she ever could have imagined. Here at the Western Sky, she discovered she loved fixing up properties and she was good at it. She had learned she could be completely focused on something when she set her mind to it and she had learned to count on herself instead of a team of handlers to take care of her every need.

Most important, she had found inside herself a strength and courage she never would have imagined before she had been forced to rely on them. She had a suspicion she wasn't finished needing those attributes. Now that she had seen him again and realized she still loved him, she knew she was going to have many days and nights of sorrow ahead.

At least she would have her daughter to help her through.

"We'll be okay, kiddo," she said again, then levered

herself up from the rocking chair, not an easy task these days.

"Come, Simone. Come, Hector." She spoke to her bichon frise and to the Lab mix Easton had talked her into a month ago. "We've got flowers to plant."

The dogs jumped up and Mimi walked down the steps after them.

Like the complicated process of maneuvering around with her pregnancy bulk, she would eventually learn how to live with this emptiness in her heart.

He awoke disoriented and with his side bellowing in pain.

Brant drew in a deep focused breath and then another and another until he could force the pain to recede enough that he could think.

He hadn't slept 'round the clock, as he might have hoped, only about ten hours. According to the lighted face of his watch, it was 5:00 a.m. At this time of year, just a few weeks after the summer solstice, the sun rose early. Out his window he could see a pale rim of light along the jagged mountain peaks, a clear indication that sunrise was an hour or so away.

He lay in bed for a long moment, catching his breath and his bearings. He was a lousy patient, as any of the nurses at the Ramstein hospital could have attested. He hated the feeling that his body could be vulnerable, that he wasn't at full fighting form.

The doctors told him he could expect a good two or three months of healing time before he felt like himself. He was ready for it to happen this minute.

He sighed. He would get over it. He was good at learning to live with things he didn't want.

Like his memories of Mimi.

He didn't want to think about her, so he swung his legs over the side of the bed and headed for the bathroom.

She had made big changes here. New light fixtures, new paint to replace the aging wallpaper, even the vanity was new.

Blasted woman. He washed his hands and headed for the kitchen for a drink of water, dressed only in low-slung sweats. He turned on the low light above the kitchen and frowned again at more evidence of Mimi's handiwork. The paint was new here, as well, and it looked to him as if the knotty pine cabinets had a new coat of stain.

He hoped like hell she hadn't paid for everything out of her own pocket, that Easton had taken care of the expenses out of the ranch maintenance account she was named on with him.

When he had his strength back a little bit, he planned to have a long talk with Easton to find out what she possibly could have been thinking to allow Mimi here.

Not that he could blame Easton for this mess. He knew from past experience that Mimi could talk her way into anything.

But why would she want to? Why was she here? None of it made sense. When she walked away that terrible last day, she had left him in no doubt that she wanted nothing to do with him.

As sweet as you've been, Brant, you're...well, not exactly my type.

She couldn't offer much more clarity than that. And yet she'd spent the past five months taking care of his ranch while she grew huge with child.

He shook his head as he turned on the faucet—a

new brushed nickel one that looked complicated and expensive. After he filled his glass, he turned around and nearly spilled the water all over the floor when he found her standing in the doorway in a nightgown, with a blanket wrapped around her shoulders.

"Mimi! What the hell?"

So much for being a highly trained commando. Mortification swamped him that she could catch him off guard like this, sore and sleepy and wearing only loose sweats.

He also had an instant of painful awareness that seeing her like this, lush and feminine and lovely in her soft mint-green nightgown, while he was only wearing sweats, would show her quite clearly just how glad at least some of him was to see her.

"Sorry. I saw the light and wanted to make sure you were okay."

"You sure moved fast from Gwen's cabin," he muttered, willing away his response.

A delicate hint of color climbed her ivory skin. "I slept on the sofa," she admitted. "I know, nervy of me. But you seemed so shaky earlier that I thought maybe I better check on you. I stopped in around midnight and…you were moaning a little in your sleep and I didn't feel right about leaving you here by yourself."

Now it was his turn to flush. He hated that the pain he fought so hard to contain during the day could growl to life when he wasn't conscious of it.

"I don't need a keeper."

He started to say more but then he caught her expression of horror and realized she was staring at his bandages, the eight-inch-wide gauze wrapped around his middle and the corresponding size encasing his arm from mid-forearm to above his elbow.

One hand fluttered to her mouth and her big green eyes filled with tears. "Oh, Brant."

He shifted. "Come on. Cut it out. Don't cry."

She drew in a ragged breath then exhaled a sobbing sort of noise, those eyes swimming with tears now, and he groaned. Though a big section of his brain was calling him any number of synonyms for nutty as a fruitcake, he crossed the distance between them and pulled her against his uninjured side.

"Come on, don't cry. I'm okay."

"You could have been killed."

"But I wasn't." He was suddenly fiercely glad of that, that he had been given one more chance to hold her again, to feel her soft curves and smell that delicious scent of flowers and citrus and her.

"I told myself not to worry, that you could take care of yourself," she whispered. "But I think I've prayed more in five months than I have the rest of my life put together and I've completely devoured all the coverage I could on Afghanistan."

Something in her words tugged at his Mimi-dazed brain, but it still took a moment for the incongruity of it to click.

"Why do you care?"

She lifted her eyes to his and he saw embarrassment flicker there and something else, something deeper, before she shifted her gaze away. "I just do."

She was lying. He knew it. He lifted her chin to face him again and this time he read everything in her eyes and the truth reached out and coldcocked him.

He stared at her for a long time and then shook his head. "You are a big fat liar, Mimi Van Hoyt."

The corners of her mouth trembled a little but she

quickly straightened it out. "I know," she said in a deceptively casual tone. "I'm so big I can barely fit through doorways these days."

"You know that's not what I meant. I think you're more beautiful than you've ever been. But you lied to me that last day. You stood here in my house and fibbed through your perfect little teeth."

She stepped away from him, taking all her heat and softness away and leaving him cold in the predawn chill. "I…don't know what you're talking about."

He thought of the five months of misery he had spent, how it had taken every ounce of hard-fought discipline he possessed to focus on the mission and not wallow in self-pity. "It was all an act to push me away, wasn't it? You didn't mean a word."

She wrapped her arms around her chest, which just made her nightgown stretch across her round belly.

"Yes, I did. I didn't—I don't—want you dragged into my world, Brant. You saw how ugly it could be and those photographers showing up here was just a small sampling of what it can be like. I love you too much to put you through that."

He stared at her, her words surging around and through him. *I love you too much.* Some corner of his mind had begun to suspect it, but hearing her say the words still stunned him like a percussion round.

"What did you say?"

"I can't put you through that. It's not fair. You're a good, honorable man. I'm Mimi Van Hoyt—stupid, rich, silly socialite. I'll ruin your life."

By the time she finished, she was nearly sobbing and he realized two things simultaneously—that she wholly believed her words, and that he had been a frigging idiot.

"It's my life. Don't you think I ought to have a say in whether it's ruined or not?"

"No." She looked as distressed as she was determined. "You don't know what it's like in the spotlight and I do."

"I don't care."

"You say that now. But you haven't had to live with it day in and day out your entire life."

"Poor Mimi." He couldn't help himself, he pulled her into his arms again.

"You don't want that, Brant. Please believe me on this."

"Hate to break it to you, Mimi, but you don't get to decide what I want and don't want."

She opened her mouth to argue, but he gave a long-suffering sigh and shut her up by kissing her. She stood rigid in his arms for a moment and then she melted against him, her arms around his neck and her belly pressing against him.

It was sweet and wonderful, better even than kicking off his boots after a two-week mission, and he never wanted it to end.

"I just spent four months missing you every single minute of every single day," he murmured against her mouth. "I fell asleep thinking about you and woke up thinking about you. It took all my concentration to do my job."

She made a tiny sound but he couldn't tell what it meant.

"I love you, Mimi. I love your stubborn streak and your funny sense of humor and your big green eyes. I love the way you chew her lip when you're concentrating and the way you pamper that silly little dog and how you shiver when I kiss you. You want to know what I want, with everything inside me? You. That's all. You. Today, tomorrow, forever."

When her eyes met his, they were dazed and a deeper green than he'd ever seen them.

"What about the media circus?"

"What about them? You said yourself they haven't bothered you much when you're living here. So we'll just spent the next fifty years being boring and they'll lose interest."

"I wish it were that easy."

He kissed her again. "Who said life was supposed to be easy? We can make it work, Mimi. I swear to you. Can't you trust me?"

This couldn't be happening. Mimi closed her eyes, wondering if this was another of those dreams where she woke up with a wet pillow and empty arms.

No. He was real. Big and solid and wonderful and claiming he loved her.

She wanted so desperately to believe him, to hold on to the delicious dream that they could actually build a life together.

If any man was strong enough to face off against the paparazzi, it was Brant. And he was right; they had quickly tired of her sedate pace of life here in Pine Gulch. What was the fun in shooting her when she wasn't doing anything outrageous, just living her life like Maura Howard would?

Could she dare believe him?

"I'm having another man's child. Are you okay with that?"

His mouth quirked up in a half smile. "The way I heard, it was in vitro fertilization."

"You know that's not true."

"As far as I'm concerned, it is." He kissed her again, leaving her no doubts that he meant his words.

A fragile hope began to quiver inside her. A life with him here in Pine Gulch or wherever his Army career took him. She wanted it, more than she'd ever wanted anything in her life.

"Are we having a boy or a girl?" Brant asked against her mouth, and just like that she started to cry again. He kissed away every tear.

She didn't deserve to be this happy, did she? As soon as the thought pulsed through her, she pushed it away. Why didn't she deserve a little happiness? Or huge bushels full of it?

"A girl." She gave him a watery smile, a smile that carried all the love in her heart for him. "I was thinking about naming her Abigail Sage. It was my grandmother's name."

"Abigail Western. Has a nice ring to it, don't you think?"

She stared at him for a long moment and finally had to force herself to breathe. A quiet peace seemed to eddy around them like the rivulets of Cold Creek, washing away all the pain, all the doubt, all the hurt. In his arms, she could believe anything was possible.

"Yes," she said softly. "I think Abigail Western sounds perfect."

Brant smiled and kissed her with a tenderness that nearly made her cry again. "If she's anything like her mother, she will be."

Mimi shook her head. She wasn't perfect. Far from it. She was a work in progress—but now she had her own blue-eyed warrior to help her on the journey.

Epilogue

"You make a beautiful bride."

Mimi hugged Easton, thinking how lovely her maid of honor looked. No one seeing this fragile, feminine creature in the pale sage dress with the long blond hair in a graceful updo would ever guess she spent most of her days riding fence line and fixing tractors.

Easton was stunning, even with that hint of sadness in her blue eyes.

"I appreciate you saying that," Mimi answered, "especially since I'm bigger than one of your cows right now."

"You glow, just like a new bride—and mom-to-be—is supposed to. Brant can't take his eyes off you."

That particular feeling was mutual. Every time she happened to see him in his dress uniform with that chest full of medals, looking tall and gorgeous and commanding, she couldn't seem to look away.

Her gaze unerringly found him speaking with his friend Quinn Southerland and Quinn's wife, Tess. Brant held their newborn son, Joe, only a month old, and he looked completely natural with a tiny bundle in his arms.

She smiled with anticipation, imagining him holding their child, and she suddenly couldn't wait.

"He's something, isn't he?"

"He is," Easton agreed. "Sometimes I want to wring his neck but I wouldn't change him."

Mimi thought of how dear the other woman had become to her in the six months since she showed up at the Western Sky, afraid and alone. Easton had become the true sister Mimi had always wanted and never found with every new step-sibling her father gave her.

When Easton turned to whisper in Mimi's ear over the noise of the music and the crowd, she leaned closer, expecting maybe a tidbit of gossip or words of encouragement.

Instead, Easton smiled for the benefit of the other wedding guests and murmured, "Screw him over, Ms. Van Hoyt, and I'll come looking for you with a cattle prod."

"I wouldn't dare," Mimi promised with a laugh. Though she knew Easton was completely serious in her threat, she also knew her friend was thrilled she and Brant had found each other. "And it's Mrs. Western now."

"Good. As long we understand each other." Easton smiled back, then changed the subject, her duties as loyal foster sister apparently discharged. "I can't believe the vultures haven't descended yet."

"Thanks for the reminder." Mimi winced. Even now, the press corps would be milling at the end of the access road to the Western Sky, where she and Brant had married a half hour ago next to the silvery creek she had driven into that first day.

She had hoped to keep the wedding a secret, but Pine Gulch was a small town. Even though their wedding was intimate, between the caterers and the band and the florist, word had somehow trickled out. The paparazzi had begun arriving the night before and some of them had even started camping out on the public right-of-way along Cold Creek Canyon Road.

"How did you keep them out?" Easton asked.

"Brant threatened them all with a shotgun again," she said.

"He did not!"

"Okay, he didn't threaten them. But he made sure he had his Remington with him and ever so subtly held on to it at his side when we went down to talk to them this morning. We promised if they wouldn't try to crash the actual ceremony, we would come down and pose for the cameras later."

She supposed it had been foolish to hope she and Brant might avoid the tabloids completely, especially since the public had avidly latched on to the story when rumors of her romance with Brant and the impending wedding started to trickle out. The pregnant society heiress and the gorgeous injured war hero made for great copy.

They would probably have to cope with paparazzi for a while, what with the wedding and her impending birth, but she had high hopes that they'd lose interest soon. Brant didn't seem to be bothered by it. In fact, he seemed to be finding great humor in their interest, for the most part—especially his new nickname, Mimi's Warrior.

She pressed a hand to her abdomen, hoping she could make it on her feet long enough for a photo session. The vague aches in her back had intensified over the past hour, but she was doing her best to ignore them.

"Uh-oh. Werner alert," Easton said. "Want me to distract him?"

Mimi shook her head. "Thanks for the offer, but I think I'll be okay."

To her shock, her father seemed as close as she'd ever seen to being pleased about something she was doing. He was actually happy about her marriage to Brant, something she never would have expected.

They both had such strong personalities, she never would have guessed they'd rub together so well. Brant hadn't tried to ingratiate himself in her father's graces. In fact, he'd been on the abrasive side, making it clear that while Werner might consider his daughter a bubbleheaded socialite, Brant had far different views. Instead of being offended, her father had treated him with respect and even admiration.

"You look just like your mother did on her wedding day," Werner said gruffly now, and she was aware that Easton, the traitor, had melted away into the crowd.

Mimi laughed. "Was she eight and a half months pregnant, too?"

"You know she wasn't. But she was almost as pretty as you are right now."

He looked at Brant, still holding baby Joe. "He's a good man. He's almost good enough for you."

"Thanks, Dad."

He paused for a long moment, and then he smiled— a little sadly, she thought. "I love you, you know. I'm not always great at showing it, but I do."

Tears welled up in her eyes but she refused to let them ruin her mascara. Not on her wedding day.

She kissed his cheek, the first time in her recent memory she had initiated affectionate contact between them. Werner stood stiffly for a long moment and then he gathered her close in a clumsy sort of hug, made even more awkward by her belly.

She closed her eyes, smelling the cologne he had created exclusively for himself at a Paris fragrance house. In this moment, all the pain of the past and the silly power struggles between them seemed far away.

"He's a good man," her father repeated. "He'll take good care of you and the baby."

Once he recovered from his initial shock at her pregnancy, Werner had once more surprised her. He seemed to actually be looking forward to becoming a grandfather.

Marta, his current wife, gestured to him a moment later and Werner gave her another awkward squeeze then went to join her stepmother.

Mimi felt the heat of someone's gaze on her and turned to find Brant watching her. She smiled at him and headed toward him, but she had only taken a few steps when she felt something strange.

She froze and it took her a full minute to figure out what had happened. When she did, she started to laugh and couldn't seem to stop.

Brant met her halfway and pulled her into his warm embrace. "I never realized being married to me would be such a laugh fest."

This set her off again and she had to wipe her eyes with the little lace-trimmed hankie Easton had given her, the something old that had belonged to Brant's foster mother, Jo Winder.

"Um, have you seen Jake?" she asked him between giggles.

He frowned. "I think I saw him and Maggie out on the dance floor a minute ago. Why?"

She wrapped her arms as tightly as she could manage around him with her bulk in the way. He obligingly leaned his head down so she could whisper in his ear.

"My water just broke."

He jerked back as if she'd punched him and she had to laugh again at his stunned expression.

"You're not due for three more weeks!"

"I guess Abigail was a little put out that we didn't wait for her to be the flower girl at her mommy and daddy's wedding. Either that or she's a bit of a prima donna and wants all the attention for herself."

He still wore that stunned expression but after a moment, it shifted to something else, a complex mix of nerves and shock, underscored by a deep joy. He pulled her into his arms again and she felt his lips on her hair for only a moment, then he loosened his hold.

"Okay. We can do this. Where's Jake? We need to get your bag from inside. It's still packed, right? I'll drive us to Idaho Falls. Or do you want to take the limousine?"

This man who could coordinate complicated troop movements and arrange logistical support to transport an entire company of soldiers across the world within a few hours looked more than a little panicked.

She smiled and squeezed his fingers. "Dr. Dalton. Let's start with him."

"Right. Jake." He stepped away to go after the doctor, then suddenly turned back to her and swept her back into his arms. He kissed her fiercely, eyes blazing with tenderness.

"I love you," he said.

She managed a smile, even as the first contraction hit. "I still don't know why, but I'm so glad you do. I love you, too."

"You're doing this just to get me out of the photo shoot, aren't you?"

More laughter bubbled out of her. "No, but I wish I'd thought of it. You know they're going to go crazy over this. Not every bride leaves her own wedding reception in labor."

"Let them go crazy. It will be a great story we can tell Abby someday." He paused. "You're going to be a fantastic mother."

"If we don't hurry, I'm afraid I'm going to become a fantastic mother in the middle of my own wedding reception."

He grinned, squeezed her hand and rushed away.

Mimi watched him go, her warrior. She thought of the journey that had led her here, the strange twists and turns. It was fate that had led her to run to Gwen that day, fate that had brought her to this ranch she loved so much. And to this man she loved more than she could believe possible.

She pressed a hand to her abdomen as she saw Brant return with Jake Dalton in tow. "We're going to be okay, kiddo," she murmured. "You, me and your wonderful daddy."

* * * * *

*Rancher Ramsey Westmoreland's temporary cook
is way too attractive for his liking.
Little does he know Chloe Burton came to his
ranch with another agenda entirely....*

That man across the street had to be, without a doubt, the most handsome man she'd ever seen.

Chloe Burton's pulse beat rhythmically as he stopped to talk to another man in front of a feed store. He was tall, dark and every inch of sexy—from his Stetson to the well-worn leather boots on his feet. And from the way his jeans and Western shirt fit his broad muscular shoulders, it was quite obvious he had everything it took to separate the men from the boys. The combination was enough to corrupt any woman's mind and had her weakening even from a distance. Her body felt flushed. It was hot. Unsettled.

Over the past year the only male who had gotten her time and attention had been the e-mail. That was simply pathetic, especially since now she was practically drooling simply at the sight of a man. Even his stance— both hands in his jeans pockets, legs braced apart, was a pose she would carry to her dreams.

And he was smiling, evidently enjoying the conversation being exchanged. He had dimples, incredibly sexy dimples in not one but both cheeks.

"What are you staring at, Clo?"

Chloe nearly jumped. She'd forgotten she had a lunch date. She glanced over the table at her best friend from college, Lucia Conyers.

"Take a look at that man across the street in the blue shirt, Lucia. Will he not be perfect for Denver's first issue of *Simply Irresistible* or what?" Chloe asked with so much excitement she almost couldn't stand it.

She was the owner of *Simply Irresistible,* a magazine for today's up-and-coming woman. Their once-a-year Irresistible Man cover, which highlighted a man the magazine felt deserved the honor, had increased sales enough for Chloe to open a Denver office.

When Lucia didn't say anything but kept staring, Chloe's smile widened. "Well?"

Lucia glanced across the booth at her. "Since you asked, I'll tell you what I see. One of the Westmorelands—Ramsey Westmoreland. And yes, he'd be perfect for the cover, but he won't do it."

Chloe raised a brow. "He'd get paid for his services, of course."

Lucia laughed and shook her head. "Getting paid won't be the issue, Clo—Ramsey is one of the wealthiest sheep ranchers in this part of Colorado. But everyone knows what a private person he is. Trust me—he won't do it."

Chloe couldn't help but smile. The man was the epitome of what she was looking for in a magazine cover and she was determined that whatever it took, he would be it.

"Um, I don't like that look on your face, Chloe. I've seen it before and know exactly what it means."

She watched as Ramsey Westmoreland entered the store with a swagger that made her almost breathless. She *would* be seeing him again.

Look for Silhouette Desire's
HOT WESTMORELAND NIGHTS
by Brenda Jackson
Available March 9
Wherever books are sold

ROMANTIC
S U S P E N S E

Sparked by Danger, Fueled by Passion.

Introducing a brand-new miniseries
Lawmen of Black Rock

Peyton Wilkerson's life shatters when her
four-month-old daughter, Lilly, vanishes.
But handsome sheriff Tom Grayson is
determined to put the pieces together and
reunite her with her baby. Will Tom be able
to protect Peyton and Lilly while fighting
his own growing feelings?

Find out in
His Case, Her Baby
by
CARLA CASSIDY

Available in March wherever books are sold

SPECIAL EDITION

FROM *USA TODAY* BESTSELLING AUTHOR
CHRISTINE RIMMER

BRAVO FAMILY TIES

A BRIDE FOR JERICHO BRAVO

Marnie Jones had long ago buried her wild-child impulses and opted to be "safe," romantically speaking. But one look at born rebel Jericho Bravo and she began to wonder if her thrill-seeking side was about to be revived. Because if ever there was a man worth taking a chance on, there he was, right within her grasp....

Available in March
wherever books are sold.

Visit Silhouette Books at www.eHarlequin.com

SSE65511

HARLEQUIN *Presents*

*Two families torn apart by secrets and desire
are about to be reunited in*

Hot Bed of Scandal

a sexy new duet by

Kelly Hunter

EXPOSED: MISBEHAVING WITH THE MAGNATE

#2905 **Available March 2010**

Gabriella Alexander returns to the French vineyard she
was banished from after being caught in flagrante with the
owner's son Lucien Duvalier—only to finish what they started!

REVEALED: A PRINCE AND A PREGNANCY

#2913 **Available April 2010**

Simone Duvalier wants Rafael Alexander and always has, but
they both get more than they bargained for when a night of
passion and a royal revelation rock their world!

HARLEQUIN
Ambassadors

Want to share your passion for reading Harlequin® Books?

Become a Harlequin Ambassador!

Harlequin Ambassadors are a group of passionate and well-connected readers who are willing to share their joy of reading Harlequin® books with family and friends.

You'll be sent all the tools you need to spark great conversation, including free books!

All we ask is that you share the romance with your friends and family!

You'll also be invited to have a say in new book ideas and exchange opinions with women just like you!

To see if you qualify* to be a Harlequin Ambassador, please visit www.HarlequinAmbassadors.com.

*Please note that not everyone who applies to be a Harlequin Ambassador will qualify. For more information please visit www.HarlequinAmbassadors.com.

Thank you for your participation.

BAP09BPA

REQUEST YOUR FREE BOOKS!

2 FREE NOVELS PLUS 2 FREE GIFTS!

SPECIAL EDITION

Life, Love and Family!

YES! Please send me 2 FREE Silhouette® Special Edition® novels and my 2 FREE gifts (gifts are worth about $10). After receiving them, if I don't wish to receive any more books, I can return the shipping statement marked "cancel." If I don't cancel, I will receive 6 brand-new novels every month and be billed just $4.24 per book in the U.S. or $4.99 per book in Canada. That's a saving of 15% off the cover price! It's quite a bargain! Shipping and handling is just 50¢ per book in the U.S. and 75¢ per book in Canada.* I understand that accepting the 2 free books and gifts places me under no obligation to buy anything. I can always return a shipment and cancel at any time. Even if I never buy another book from Silhouette, the two free books and gifts are mine to keep forever.

235 SDN E4NC 335 SDN E4NN

Name _____ (PLEASE PRINT) _____

Address _____ Apt. # _____

City _____ State/Prov. _____ Zip/Postal Code _____

Signature (if under 18, a parent or guardian must sign)

Mail to the Silhouette Reader Service:
IN U.S.A.: P.O. Box 1867, Buffalo, NY 14240-1867
IN CANADA: P.O. Box 609, Fort Erie, Ontario L2A 5X3

Not valid for current subscribers to Silhouette Special Edition books.

Want to try two free books from another line?
Call 1-800-873-8635 or visit www.morefreebooks.com.

* Terms and prices subject to change without notice. Prices do not include applicable taxes. N.Y. residents add applicable sales tax. Canadian residents will be charged applicable provincial taxes and GST. Offer not valid in Quebec. This offer is limited to one order per household. All orders subject to approval. Credit or debit balances in a customer's account(s) may be offset by any other outstanding balance owed by or to the customer. Please allow 4 to 6 weeks for delivery. Offer available while quantities last.

Your Privacy: Silhouette is committed to protecting your privacy. Our Privacy Policy is available online at www.eHarlequin.com or upon request from the Reader Service. From time to time we make our lists of customers available to reputable third parties who may have a product or service of interest to you. If you would prefer we not share your name and address, please check here. ☐

Help us get it right—We strive for accurate, respectful and relevant communications. To clarify or modify your communication preferences, visit us at www.ReaderService.com/consumerchoice.

SSE10